T0098320

COME AND
JOIN THE DANCE

COME AND
JOIN THE DANCE

JOYCE JOHNSON

OPEN ROAD

INTEGRATED MEDIA

NEW YORK

Copyright © 1961 by Joyce Glassman

Cover design by Drew Padrutt

ISBN 978-1-4804-8133-6

This edition published in 2014 by Open Road Integrated Media, Inc.
345 Hudson Street
New York, NY 10014
www.openroadmedia.com

COME AND
JOIN THE DANCE

CHAPTER ONE

A WEEK BEFORE, the privet hedges had been shorn, but the fences were still standing. And a green wooden wall shut the college off from the street where cars, unseen, rushed and moaned past. The world remained in order. Two old men marched decorously behind lawn mowers on the vast lawn that would soon be trod to death at Commencement.

The steel grillwork on the gymnasium windows divided the lawn, the old men, into squares. It was possible to find the precise number of squares to an old man. Susan counted eighteen. The Melville question was still to be answered though, and thinking about anything else was wasting time. The examination would be over at twelve, and it was eleven-thirty. There were sixty-three girls in the gymnasium. They were all on Melville. Susan wondered what Melville would have thought of sixty-three girls concentrating on him at once.

Sixty-two—she could not concentrate, although she had repeated "Melville" to herself so often that the name had decomposed. She had become frozen into a deadly laziness. If she moved she would shatter like glass.

A while ago, she had watched, far off, the smooth running of her mind, and had thought, I am doing that, but could not really believe it. But this was before she had forgotten to care about doing well. Elizabethan Shakespeare, Pre-Romantic Blake, Classical Pope, Romantic Keats—they had all been caught; pinned, labeled and laid dead upon the paper. Now there was only Melville to deal with—the last question in the Comprehensive Examination in English Literature, which was the last examination she would ever take. She had expected the occasion to be a kind of ceremony. At twelve o'clock, a heavy black line would be drawn and freedom would happen to her; there would be a life without examinations, no more childhood. But now she could feel none of the excitement of knowing that something was happening for the last time. This was probably because she was tired—she had stayed up studying until four in the morning; the excitement would come at twelve, she supposed. She wanted it to be twelve immediately. Melville was unimportant and all the other questions were unimportant and had nothing to do with what really was going to happen.

She found herself getting up from her chair and walking to the proctor's desk, placing her paper on it—unfinished. It was only twenty to twelve. But the doors of the gymnasium swung behind her. The hall outside with its marble floor was cool and smelled of soap. She had begun to walk very quickly. She wanted to run, but that might have looked peculiar. As it was, the loud click of her heels embarrassed her. There was a sign up: QUIET PLEASE, AN EXAMINATION IS TAKING PLACE.

Outside, there was the sun and the bewildering, heavy smell of the cut grass, while beyond the green wall everything was moving much too fast in the street. She wondered why she had been in such a hurry, because there was really nothing to do but wait for twelve, after all—she had a date then with Jerry. He had insisted on seeing her, even though she had told him that she had always expected to be alone in her first hour of freedom. Of course, that had only been another one of her gestures, like running out before the examination was over. Jerry didn't understand gestures. Sometimes she felt that he had an unbearably literal mind.

I don't want to see him, she thought. There seemed to be something else she wanted to do, but she was too lazy to think of it. The laziness began to turn into pain, and she decided to go up to her room and change her dress, comb her hair. That would take up another twenty minutes.

The wall that ran around the college was flimsy, easily destroyed. One night a year, in fact, the fraternity boys from Columbia surged across Broadway, shouting and singing, and demolished it. This was a ritual. The girls would leave their beds and stand watching by their windows. As each green plank crashed, they would laugh harshly, uncertainly. There would always be one bold-voiced girl who would taunt the invaders: "Why don't you come up? What are you afraid of?" This would be answered by laughter and an eager cry of "Hey! What floor are you on?"

The boys never came up; when the wall was down, they would walk away, almost casually. The girls would one by one put out their lights, listening tensely as long as the laughter in the streets lasted. Then it would be quiet again. In the morning, there would be the sound of hammering. The boys paid for the new wall, of course—this was part of the ritual.

Beyond the wall, to the west, was the park and beyond that, the river. In the daytime, the park was noisy with children, and in the circle of benches around the fountain there were always the same old ladies sitting with black-gloved, restless hands. There were other places, as one went deeper into the park, where the bushes grew close and heavy and couples lay in the long, soot-stained grass. This was the area named "Down Below"—to the girls in the college it was a miniature wilderness, and it was some-what of an adventure to be led by a young man down into it on a Saturday night, remembering the housemother's warnings that there were "incidents" there as well as rats.

No one from the college ever went down to the river. Occasionally a child was killed trying to dodge the speeding cars on the highway that ran beside it. And now and then, bums came to sun themselves on the strip of dirty grass that the park provided as a riverbank and tried to catch the polluted fish. The river was dark, foul. From the distance, it looked blue and could be admired from the west windows of the college. It was pleasant to watch the ships sailing past with all the little dots on them that weren't really people.

In ten more days Susan would be on a ship. She was going to Paris. Six months ago she had cashed in the bonds her grandmother had left in her name and made her reservations—it had seemed the thing to do. "Isn't it incredible!" she would cry when she talked about it. "Incredible" was one of her favorite words. So was "strange." She had learned to say them with just the right amount of breath and wistfulness. Once a boy had said to her, "I love the way you always wonder at things," and this had embarrassed Susan—it implied an innocence she knew she did not have. But the words came too readily, were too convenient to give up. And they really did describe the world as seen from a distance. She was detached, which was more sophisticated than being innocent, and therefore something to be proud of. So she continued to say, "I felt strange," rather than "I felt sad," and a great deal of what she saw around her was also "strange," and she knew that after she had sailed on the incredible ship to Paris, she would find that Paris was incredible, too.

When she came into her room, she realized suddenly that she had been erased from it. She had not noticed it that morning when, before the examination, she had shipped the last of her books home to Cedarhurst. For weeks there had been an urgency in her to leave, to leave immediately, to rush toward the day when she would drive off in a taxi with her last suitcase, putting the college behind her. Now her pictures were taken down, and even most of her clothes were packed. It was too late to stop herself from moving. The room proved that she was going away. Only the maple furniture would remain, the same furniture the college loaned to each student. Next fall an unknown girl would come to take her place, sleep in her bed. She remembered Mr. Davidson, her advisor, complacently saying that the students never changed—the faces were the same semester after semester, the same things were said, thought, done. That had been a year ago. She had railed at him furiously: "People have no right to exist if they're replaceable." He had smiled and said, "Well . . . my, my." The rage had left her, and she had felt foolish. Now she felt replaceable as well—she was somehow no longer living anywhere. Outside her room, her trunks stood in the corridor with all the other trunks. They were very new and black and solid; in a week they would leave with her. Perhaps if she lived anywhere at all now it was with them—she and her trunks sitting in the corridor, waiting out a week that had not been accounted for.

She heard the bell ring in the gymnasium, and moments afterward the bright voices of girls on the path to the dormitory. It was twelve o'clock. She looked out of her window and saw Jerry on the porch. He was always on time. I'm late, she thought guiltily. She was always late for appointments—she had a horror of waiting.

As she stared at him through the window now, Jerry suddenly became someone she didn't know—a boy with light brown hair wearing a brown jacket, slouched against one of the white limestone pillars. Everything was so much easier when you abstracted someone. She could almost say "I love you" to the boy on the porch who was too far away to hear her; she wasn't able to say it to Jerry. Lately, she couldn't bear the way he waited for those words, his eyes blinking behind their glass lenses, his face positively yellow with unhappiness. "I love you," he would say to her, and she would have to change the subject, tell him not to take things so seriously. Perhaps she simply ought to lie to him—after all, I'm going away, she thought. The terrifying thing about Jerry was that he was someone she could marry—she could marry him and never have to go alone to Paris—he was only waiting for a signal.

The boy on the porch looked up, spotted her at the window and began to wave. She was supposed to wave back. But she didn't want to. It would only be her hand flopping in the air and it wouldn't mean anything. . . . But she didn't want to.

He called to her. The window wasn't open; the word came blurred through the glass and sounded a little like her name. Then he began to wave so frantically that it embarrassed her to watch him. Her hands felt peculiarly cold. She moved away from the window. She had taken a freshly ironed dress from the closet; now she put it back and lay down upon her bed.

In a little while, the telephone in the corridor began to ring. It rang about ten times, stopped, then started to ring again, but none of the other girls were around, and she was too lazy to answer it. When the ringing stopped, there was a terrible stillness in the room. She wanted to fall asleep.

At two o'clock she went down into the street, out beyond the green wall. There were so many mirrors on Broadway. Her image floated ahead of her like a balloon, hovering in the windshields of cars, appearing transparent, ghostlike, in the glass doors of Henry's Pharmacy, blue and elongated in the chrome façade of the Riverside Café. She walked briskly, as though she had an appointment, and was careful to turn her head as little as possible. It was agony to be caught looking into mirrors.

People were so eager to detect vanity, to embarrass the vain: "Hey, stop looking at yourself once in a while. You look all right." She knew she looked "all right." She had an orderly enough face, although not one she would have chosen. It was too round for her taste and had green eyes in it and a short, straight nose. Her hair hung long, straight down the sides of her face, and was reddish brown. Whenever people told her she was pretty, she was a little surprised and wanted to ask them whether this was really true, but she was always able to manage a short, breathless laugh just in time. Somehow she never quite expected anyone to have thoughts about her—it was rather frightening to discover that you existed behind your own back.

What did others see when they looked at her? She would try to study her face as though it belonged to someone else. This was not vanity—she knew that. If you were truly vain, you were certain of what you saw, certain enough to love your image, delight in it. But her face cheated her. It had a way of rearranging itself when she looked into mirrors, as though it were giving a performance. She would feel her eyebrows rising slightly, her eyes widening, her mouth pinching at the corners as if it were trying to look smaller. The image in the glass always had the same perfect, terrifying blandness. It did not belong to her. Her face could not look that way.

If she could only rush past an infinity of mirrors, she might catch a glimpse of her face someday before it had a chance to freeze. Perhaps it would appear before her for an instant when she turned a corner on a street, or when she raced down a flight of stairs. She would recognize it immediately, even though she had never seen it, and would accept its beauty or ugliness. But it would not be bland. She wondered if she could ever run fast enough.

CHAPTER TWO

SHE HAD WALKED the six blocks to 110th Street and seen no one, although she had even—but only out of habit because she did not really want to meet anyone—looked into all the windows of the luncheonettes and peered into the gloom of the Riverside Café, where the floor was being mopped and all the chairs were standing on the tables. It was two o'clock, and of course people would not come out for coffee until four and it was much too early for beer. She would have to be alone this afternoon. That might even be what she wanted. In fact, when she had passed Schulte's she had seen a girl at the counter with Kay's ragged dark hair and dirty raincoat and had not gone in. It was odd not wanting to talk to Kay—she would understand something like not being able to wave back at someone who was waving at you. "All right," she would shrug, "so you did it. It's done." Kay's acceptance would have absolved her; maybe all the brown-haired, spectacled, thin young men on the street would have ceased to look like Jerry. But Schulte's was two blocks behind her now. Should she continue walking downtown, or should she cross Broadway here as she always did and walk the six blocks back to the college on the other side of the street? I have habits, she thought bitterly, like an old woman.

She wondered what habits she would develop in Paris. Perhaps Paris would be big enough to get lost in. She had always had a horror of losing herself in unfamiliar streets. New York was a comfortable size—only six blocks long.

It had often amused her that there were no photographs of these six blocks in the brochure the college sent to prospective students. "New York will be your classroom, your laboratory," the writer promised. Susan remembered how avidly she had studied that brochure four years ago, sitting in her little pink room in Cedarhurst. She had been almost seventeen and had taken every word of it very seriously, wondering if she would ever have the tailored ease of those girls in the photographs, smiling in front of paintings in art galleries, smiling outside theaters before curtain time, smiling against the skyline. New York was to become hers when she started college. She would know more of it than its department stores and the Radio City Music Hall; she would no longer have to catch the five-o'clock Long Island train and be back in her parents' dining room in time for dinner.

She hadn't known that her New York would be even smaller than Cedarhurst—six blocks that had no scenic interest. Susan remembered seeing them for the first time—a grayness of drugstores, butcher shops, luncheonettes, bars, laundries—it had hardly seemed worth the effort to learn her way through them. But the streets had since taken on color, had slowly accumulated layers of significance. By now they even had an odd glamour. Susan wondered what she would find if she ever came back—

perhaps there would only be grayness again, as though Broadway had faded.

She pictured herself someday saying ruefully to a faceless, bored young man: "It's really a depressing place, isn't it? What on earth did people do there?" Perhaps by then it might be difficult to remember, or necessary to pretend not to. She had often, without being able to stop herself, chipped off little pieces of her past and added other little pieces—a fascinating game but the meaning of it had begun to scare her. What if you lived your entire life completely without urgency? You went to classes, you ate your meals, on Saturday nights a boy you didn't love took you to the movies; now and then you actually had a conversation with someone. The rest of the time—the hours that weren't accounted for—you spent waiting for something to happen to you; when you were particularly desperate you went out looking for it, you spent an evening in the Riverside Café, you walked down to 110th Street.

This year she had found herself taking certain risks—especially after Kay had quit school and moved out of the dorms into the Southwick Arms Hotel. She had kept library books out for months, she had handed in her term papers late, she had cut a dangerous number of gym classes—it was all very unnecessary, but something had made her want the feeling of living a little close to the edge; perhaps she had chosen to feel frightened rather than feel nothing at all. For the last two months she hadn't picked up her Student Mail. She was somehow unable to. She knew what would be in it—notices of events that had already taken place, terse administrative warnings: "... the books you borrowed on 2/25 are now overdue . . . you have not paid your assembly fine . . . you have not registered for tennis . . ." Perhaps there was even one note that began, "You have not picked up your Student Mail for some time." It had been sort of a private joke at first; now it was a secret source of terror. She would go out of her way to avoid meeting the postmistress—Mrs. Prosser, with her spectacles dangling genteelly from a ribbon, and her timeless gray dresses, and her sad, disdainful puzzlement over any behavior that was out of the ordinary. Why should she be afraid of Mrs. Prosser? Why should she have to make "plans" to pick up her mail some vague day when Mrs. Prosser was not on duty? She would have to confront her before graduation. There was only one week left now. . . .

Should she go uptown? Should she go downtown? She had no reason, no desire to go in either direction.

All around her people were being carried to their destinations. There was a stout man on the corner shouting, "Taxi! Taxi!"; busses stopped to absorb passengers; the subway rumbled beneath her feet; and each pedestrian was marching to an unknown, inevitable door. She was the only one in the street who walked aimlessly—except for the young man a few feet ahead of her, who was waiting now for the light to change.

She had watched him for several blocks. He had paused at every newsstand to read the same headlines, had lingered in front of shop windows that couldn't possibly have interested him, and he too had methodically peered into all the luncheonettes. He had a loping, undecided walk, and a head that hung forward as if it were too heavy for his shoulders. She felt a curious tenderness for him, for the back of his head, at least—she had not seen his face, but perhaps if he turned around they would recognize each other. Sometimes you came face to face with someone you didn't know, yet found yourself and the stranger exchanging a look of recognition. It seemed wasteful that she and this unknown young man were not walking together. Soon he would be across 110th Street, and she would be walking on the other side of Broadway back to the college, since after all there was no other place to go. But she wanted to see his face. She almost cried out to him, "Turn around, please!"

Just before the light changed, she saw him step forward as a car swerved around the corner. He stepped back almost casually and watched the car disappear. It was then that he turned toward her and she realized he was someone she knew—Kay's friend, Peter. Kay had met him just a few weeks before she left school, and lately she seemed always to be going over to his apartment. Susan found herself running to catch up with him.

"Hello!" she called loudly. "Hello, Peter!" When he turned, he had the look of someone startled out of sleep. "I'm just taking a walk," she said, feeling unbearably foolish. Why was he studying her so gravely? Could he tell that she had been running? "Somehow I always meet people on Broadway."

He smiled at her uncertainly. "I'm just taking a walk myself. Where are you headed?" he asked.

She shrugged and laughed a little, feeling that she would choke if she answered him.

"Would you like some coffee?" he said.

"Oh . . . " she said. "Well, yes."

He had an amused look—she must have sounded awfully eager. "How about the College Inn? Is that all right?"

"That's fine," she said.

They turned and began to walk back uptown. There was a silence between them that contented her, although she usually found silence uncomfortable, a kind of failure, especially if she was with someone she did not know very well. She barely knew Peter, although she knew a lot about him because of all the things Kay had told her. Kay had taken her to some of his parties, and a few times when she had met Kay at the Riverside, Peter had sat at their table. Yet she had scarcely spoken to him. This was the first time they had ever been alone together.

When they passed Schulte's Kay was still there, sitting all by herself at the counter. Susan almost said, "Oh, look—there's Kay," but without quite knowing why, she didn't; the silence was left intact. When they were halfway up the block she wondered whether Kay had seen them pass, not that Kay would have minded—she was beautifully unpossessive of people, and just because she talked about Peter so much, it didn't mean that she was in love with him; Kay had never said so. . . . Why should she have the uneasy feeling that she had done something wrong?

They were the only customers in the College Inn. They sat down in a booth near the window, considered the menu and ordered coffee. For a while, Peter stared at her across the table. His eyes were gray, deep-set, almost blank at times. His mouth was very thin when he wasn't smiling.

"Susan," Peter said abruptly, "do you have a quarter?"

"I think so."

"Well, find it. We can have some music."

She began to search through her pocketbook obediently, as though young men had always asked her for quarters, and she heard Peter impatiently beating out a private rhythm on the table. "Here's one," she said at last, dropping it into his hand.

"Excellent." He walked to the jukebox, read the titles of all the songs, then turned to her. "What would you like to hear?"

"I don't know."

"Are you being polite when you say that, or don't you care?"

Was he attacking her? She had a moment of panic. "I guess I don't care."

"It's your quarter," he said in mock reproach. "But since you're not interested, you're at my mercy." He pressed three buttons and walked back to the booth. There was a roll of jungle drums over the loudspeaker, then a woman began to shout ferociously about love. "Don't you like music?" Peter asked anxiously. They both began to laugh. "Listen, Susan," he said, "I'm completely broke. I can't even pay for your coffee. Does that matter?"

"Oh, I can pay for everything," she found herself saying.

"My check probably came yesterday, but I haven't been back to the apartment yet. I spent all my money on gasoline." He sounded apologetic, defensive, as if she had asked him for an explanation.

"I've really got lots of money," Susan said.

"You're young—you don't have a mailbox full of bills." His laugh was bitter. "I don't know why I came back to New York this time," he said.

"You've been away?"

"Oh, I disappeared for a few days—I do that now and then."

"Where do you go when you disappear?"

"This time I went to Chicago. . . . You've never seen my car, have you?"

"I don't think so," she said.

"Well, you ought to come and see it. It's beautiful. A big black Packard—1938. It's the only beautiful thing I own. It's starting to fall apart now." He sounded very sad when he said that; the car seemed to be more than just a car to him. "I should have made this trip a long one—God, I felt like it!"

"Why didn't you?" she asked shyly.

He took a cigarette out of his pack and lit it. "No money, for one thing," he said in a flat voice. "Obligations—I'm supposed to finish my thesis next semester. I can't keep getting checks from home for the rest of my life."

"Are you almost finished?" she asked.

"I've been 'almost finished' for the last five years."

"Maybe you don't want to finish. I mean, maybe you don't want to find out what's going to happen to you next. . . . " Peter was silent. She felt terribly embarrassed. Why on earth had she said that to him?—he was someone she hardly knew.

But then he said, "Maybe I don't," and she could tell he wasn't angry. He leaned toward her across the table with a sudden eagerness. "You know, Susan, I've never heard you say anything before. You come to my parties with Kay, you sit on the sofa, you listen to someone very dutifully, and every now and then you tell a story or a little joke—and that's all."

She laughed painfully. His description was accurate. "Isn't that enough?"

"I don't know—is it? Is it enough for you?"

Carefully, she folded her paper napkin into a triangle. "I really don't want this conversation," she said.

"Of course you don't," she heard him say.

"I don't see why everybody has to be so terribly warm and interested in everyone they meet just because they're afraid they'll be caught being trivial."

"But is that what we're doing?" he said quietly.

"I don't know." She had a feeling of helplessness, of vast ignorance. "I never really know whether or not I mean what I'm saying anyway."

"By the time you're my age you'll know even less."

"Your age! You're not that much older than I am."

"I'll be thirty in October."

"*You* thirty?" She laughed in disbelief.

"I thought you knew," he said.

She realized that of course she had known it all along—Peter's age, a piece of information. She had taken it for granted and then forgotten it, perhaps when she had seen him talking politics excitedly with Anthony Leone, who was only eighteen, or when he had been a little drunk at a party once and had done a crazy, disorganized dance in the middle of the room to please a girl and then had followed her around saying, "Listen now, don't be that way," while the girl giggled nervously. She looked at him again now and saw that he was indeed almost thirty; his face was hollower than Jerry's would be for many years. She remembered

Kay telling her that Peter had once been married; she remembered hearing someone refer to him as "that perpetual student." Five years was a long time to work on a thesis. There was a desk in his living room with piles of manuscript and journals on it, all thick with dust.

Peter was grinning. "Susan . . . stop looking grim. We're all getting older. But I'm going to be a promising young man as long as possible. If you haven't got all the time in the world, what else is there?"

For a moment she wanted to challenge him: "How much time does anyone really have?" But she knew that he had probably long ago rejected his own excuses, that he must be bitterly aware that the people who came to the university were a little younger every fall.

"You see through all this?" he said wryly.

She shook her head. "I see it."

"You'll be thirty someday."

"Today I had my last examination," she said. "I keep telling myself school's over, now something else begins. But nothing's any different. I haven't *changed*. Maybe I never will. When I was eight, I used to look forward to being twenty. Now I'm twenty and I'm still the same person. I really am. I may even be the same at thirty."

"You have no patience," he said.

"Well, what if there's nothing to look forward to!"

"Maybe there isn't." His voice was quiet. "No point in getting upset."

"I think you have to get upset!" She realized, astonished, that she had almost been shouting.

He got up from the table and stood beside her, putting his hand on her shoulder. "You're a nice girl," he said. "You're worth saving."

"But who's going to save me?"

"Not me," he said cheerfully. "Thank God!"

"Peter, what will I be when I'm thirty?"

"Anything," he said. "Anything you want."

CHAPTER THREE

SHE SPENT THE REST OF THE afternoon with Peter. He borrowed four dollars from her and they left the College Inn and went all around the neighborhood paying off his debts; he retrieved his shirts from the laundry, his shoes from the shoemaker, and redeemed his library card. Susan followed him happily, never bothering to ask, "Where are we going now, Peter?" For this afternoon, at least, her life had been absorbed by his, and yet at the same time, everything was peculiarly important, peculiarly distinct—the pyramids of oranges in a grocery window, the names on the marquee of the Nemo movie theater, and Peter calling, "Here cats! Here cats!" in a cracked, plaintive voice, until the thin gray cat that had been eying them crept under a car and they both laughed helplessly. She thought she would remember that forever, and the faces of the people in e streets would also be remembered and exactly how warm the sun was on her shoulders, and the fact that on 114th Street Peter grabbed her hand for an instant, saying "Wait! Look at that!" and there on the sidewalk had been a wonderfully elaborate chalk drawing of a neckless man on a lopsided horse.

The afternoon ended in a secondhand bookstore. "Let's stop in here for a minute," he had said; for the next hour he had restlessly searched the shelves for something he wanted. "There must be a book. I have to buy a book," he cried. "You help me now." She had ransacked stacks of books for him until her eyes smarted from the dust. "Let me know when you've had it," he called to her once, and she had replied gaily, "But you don't really give a damn."

Then all at once it was over. "It's five o'clock," he announced soberly.

"Oh, what will we do now?" she asked.

"I have to go back," he said. "I have to go back to the apartment."

She felt perilously close to having the words "Don't go" wrenched from her, but knew you could never say things like that and said only, "I see," because that was meaningless.

"I'm sorry. . . . You see—I have an application for a fellowship due at five tomorrow. I've been avoiding it all semester, but I ought to try to get it done. . . . Funny—I actually feel a little like working now." They stood before each other in silence, awkwardly. "So . . ." he sighed at last.

"You didn't buy a book," she reminded him crisply.

"Couldn't have anyway. I've spent all your money." They laughed. Their eyes caught for a moment as they walked out of the store into the street. "So long." He grinned at her painfully and she found that his hand had somehow captured hers. Then he let it go and began to stride down the block, disappearing at last around the corner.

Standing by herself outside the bookstore, she suddenly discovered that she could stand still in the street if she wanted to, that aimlessness could have its own legality. If she wanted to, she would walk five times around the block or take a subway downtown to no place in particular. There was no shame then in accepting temporary shelters. She walked back up Broadway to the college.

As soon as she had pushed open the green gate, she saw Jerry. He was sitting on the concrete steps outside Brooks Hall, a copy of the *New Yorker* open on his lap. She wondered how long he had been staring at the same page.

She was not at all surprised to see him, but thought, Of course. Of course he's here. He had expected her to come; she had expected to find him. If there had been no one waiting for her on the steps, she would very likely have rushed into the lobby and asked the girl at the desk hadn't there been any calls, hadn't anyone come and then gone away. And yet she was as angry with him as if he had cheated her of something.

"Hello, Jerry."

"Susan!" He scrambled to his feet, trying to jam the *New Yorker* into the pocket of his jacket. She wondered why and almost asked him. He was frantically grinning at her.

"I took a walk," she said finally, feeling that there was nothing they could say to each other that would be appropriate; anything would be hopelessly out of context.

"I figured."

"Have you been waiting long?"

"No. Not long. Not long at all," he said. But he couldn't quite look at her.

"You didn't have to wait. You could have called."

He was silent. For a moment his eyes searched hers anxiously. "I wanted to see you!" he cried.

She felt a sudden relief that he hadn't lied to her, that he hadn't said, "Well, I just thought I'd sit here and read." She wondered why she always underestimated Jerry. "I didn't think you'd want to," she said lamely.

"I thought we'd talk."

"I don't want to talk, Jerry! I really don't."

"Okay," he said sadly. "We won't talk. Shall I go away?"

"I don't know."

He took off his glasses and rubbed them against the sleeve of his jacket and tried to smile at her. Why hadn't someone warned him not to wait?

"Listen," he said, "let me take you to dinner. You don't want to eat dinner with a lot of girls."

"Jerry . . . you're terribly nice." She felt herself trapped by his niceness.

He caught her by the shoulders. "Let's go downtown. We'll really go out. We'll go to some great place, some French place, anything you like."

Should she get dressed up, go downtown with him? She could wear her black Shantung dress, which was the one dress she owned that made her feel worldly, and the long silver earrings her mother had given her. Jerry would inevitably tell her that she looked like the 1920s and they would drink cocktails and be very gay. Maybe she could be gay if she made the effort. "Will you buy me champagne?" she asked.

"We'll get drunk," he announced extravagantly. "That's what we'll do."

"All right. Let's get drunk."

He laughed uncertainly. "You know, we could. There's no school tomorrow."

"There's no more school at all!" She flung the words at him. "And I meant it about getting drunk."

"Okay," he said, bewildered.

The listlessness of the afternoon settled heavily upon her again, and she knew she could be neither gay, nor kind, nor cruel—only blank, a spectator of herself, immensely bored. She told Jerry she had to go upstairs for a little while; at least there would be no one to talk to there, she thought.

"Why?" he demanded anxiously.

"To get dressed." As good an excuse as any.

"But you look okay. . . . "

"I have to get dressed up if you're taking me out." Already her hand was pressed against the heavy glass door. "I'll be just a minute!" she called over her shoulder.

"Susan!" he cried out.

Susan turned. "Well?" she asked impatiently.

"Don't forget to come down." He looked so small and frightened. Perhaps if he had not been waiting for her, she would have telephoned him when she had come back to her room—not to apologize, but to talk. Somehow she would have managed to be great, just great. She wondered sadly why she was always being deprived of her greatness. "Of course I'll come down," she said.

It was seven o'clock when they got off the Fifth Avenue bus at 57th Street—a soft evening. The city seemed deserted, except for a few couples strolling languidly down the avenue. Susan wondered where all the afternoon people had vanished—to cocktail parties perhaps, or the icy darkness of bars; surely they were all doing something infinitely graceful, not just lingering at a bus stop because they had no idea where to go next. Across the street, the mannequins in their summer dresses stood in the muted light of the Bonwit Teller windows, their wooden limbs twisted into an impossible, infuriating sophistication. "Just look at them!" Susan cried. "They are all waiting for taxis."

Jerry very tentatively touched her arm with the tips of his fingers. "Okay," he said. "When we know where we're going, we'll go there in a taxi."

Quite unaccountably, tears had come into her eyes. "Oh, Jerry," she said, "that's ridiculous."

"No," he insisted. "I can afford it tonight. I feel like spending money. Sometimes I want to ride in taxis too."

"I thought you were so practical," she teased him.

"I'm not practical at all," he said gloomily. "I've just been broke all my life."

It was true. She remembered his home suddenly, the worn, ugly furniture arranged in the cramped rooms just as it had undoubtedly been arranged twenty years before. "You have no idea how much cheaper good things used to be," Jerry's mother had said to her. Everything his family owned was a bargain—their apartment, their car, the food they ate. "The butcher down the block is eight cents less a pound. Cashmere sweaters for five dollars if you look hard on the East Side. Movies are twenty cents less in the afternoon." His father had told her that if she and Jerry got married, he would give them the still-good-as-new bedroom set. "Isn't Dad just great!" Jerry had cried. She had only been able to smile politely, and Jerry had accused her later of a lack of warmth. Perhaps he had been right. There was nothing wrong with people who didn't have much money making ends meet and being proud of it. There was nothing wrong with people who couldn't afford taxis.

She burrowed her head into Jerry's shoulder and felt him put his arm firmly around her waist. "Hey—what's with you?"

"I'm such a snob, Jerry," she whispered. "I'm such an awful snob, I can't stand it."

"It's one of your crazy moods," he said.

"It's not a mood, it's the way I am. I'm a snob."

He laughed uncertainly.

"You shouldn't have brought me down here," she said. "This part of the city always kills me. It's all made of money. I don't mean money in the bank, but money like Henry James people had it, money so you could be really cool and never have to worry about carfare."

"I've got twenty dollars in my pocket right now," he said. "And I don't care if I get rid of all of it. How's that for coolness?"

"I wish you wouldn't spend it on me, Jerry."

"Look," he said, "I'm taking you out. I want us to have an evening. It's the end of exams and we're celebrating. Is there anything wrong with that?"

"No. I guess not."

He was holding her hand very tightly. "Hey," he murmured. "Hey there." It was his evening too. He was entitled to it. She tried to smile at him reassuringly.

The sky was growing paler, and the sun made great red shadows on the empty buildings. It was all so quiet. The elevators had stopped, and the typewriters and the telephones, yet she felt a thousand faces watching her from the darkness behind the windows. In two more weeks every street would be a street she didn't know. She was suddenly glad Jerry was with her; she moved closer to him. But when he began to kiss her, she could not shut her eyes.

CHAPTER FOUR

THE WOMEN WERE all so sleek. They are the adults, Susan thought, looking with wonder at their impeccably sheathed bodies, their bare, slender arms faintly tan a month before summer. She listened to their soft laughter and saw how easily the men leaned toward them across the little tables. "A great place," Jerry had said an hour ago, as the waiter led them across the thick carpeting to a table from which they could see everything. Thinking guiltily that what she saw was beautiful, she had found herself perversely saying, "I wonder why they've turned out all the lights," which was such a childish remark—not cool, not sleek—but she was determined not to be impressed. Restaurants were not beautiful. And she knew that the people were not really great—they put their coiffures up in curlers, worried about their charge accounts, had their feelings hurt, and were probably having dull conversations—still she wished she were completely taken in. Life was simpler for people like Jerry; they said what they meant, and they walked into strange places as themselves and said it, not wanting to be anyone else. They would always be tourists, carrying their cameras to cathedrals, staring at the natives with delight and open curiosity, half blind perhaps, but doggedly proud of their own identities. They were probably quite comfortable that way— they did not see the world as a magnificent party to which they had not been invited. And there was a certain dignity in being a tourist, if you never tried to be anything else, if you did not even dress yourself up in appropriate costumes. The black dress did not make her sleek; she was betrayed by the wisps of hair that clung to her forehead, the slight wrinkle in her left stocking, the smudge of soot across her wrist, the tightness of her lips, and by her consciousness of it all. She was a pretender.

"You still haven't told me about the exam," Jerry said. He was beginning to sound angry. He had patiently set up one conversation after another and she had evaded each with an "I don't know" or "It isn't very important, is it?"

"Oh, it was very boring," she said, knowing how annoyed he'd be. Exams, marks, were life and death to him. "In fact"— she felt pleasantly wicked—"I walked out on the American Lit question."

"You mean you couldn't answer it!" He looked so worried.

"I just got tired of sitting there," she said. "I had enough points."

"Suppose you didn't! I mean, why are you always taking risks like that? Don't you care what happens to you?"

"But I've never gotten into any trouble."

"That's amazing," Jerry said grimly. "All the classes you've cut! Did you go to gym once last term?"

"Once or twice." He would really be shocked, she thought, if he knew she hadn't picked up her mail, but she couldn't quite bring herself to tell him about that. "If you were the Dean, I bet you'd expel me."

"How were the other questions?" he asked stiffly.

"Do you want a complete breakdown on each one?"

"I don't give a damn," he said. "Sorry to have bothered you."

She began to laugh. "You didn't bother me. Oh Jerry . . . don't be bitter." She placed her hand delicately on his arm.

"I guess you find me boring too."

She picked up a lump of sugar and carefully examined the words on its paper wrapping—*La Lune d'Argent, La Lune d'Argent*. She did not look at Jerry. At last she said, "Let's get out of here and do something."

"We haven't had coffee yet," he said.

"Let's have it somewhere else."

"We might just as well have it here. It's paid for."

"You remind me," she said wearily, "of a little boy kicking a can down the street."

He was staring at her with a peculiar earnestness. "Well . . . maybe that's what I am."

"For heaven's sake, don't agree with me!" she cried. "Tell me to go to hell or something!"

"I don't understand you at all."

"Tell me to go to hell. Go on—do it."

He shook his head sadly. "I can't."

"I think we should fight, have a big scene—right here. Let's see what happens. You throw the salt shaker at me, I'll throw the sugar bowl at you. *Something!*"

"Look," he said, "I don't want to fight with you. I love you."

"But Jerry, that has nothing to do with it."

"I love you," he said, "I really love you." His hand clenched around her fingers. It was unfair, she thought. He was waiting for an answer. She nearly wept from helplessness.

"I don't know," she said painfully. "I think you're trying to make me into some sort of monster."

"But what are you talking about!" he shouted. "What do you want me to do? Okay, I wish I hated you. I wanted to hate you this afternoon when you stood me up."

"I didn't stand you up," she said, "because I didn't mean it that way. I felt strange."

"All right. I don't care what it was. But look, when you didn't come down—I tried to think, Well, if that's the way she feels about it . . . I tried to be angry with you for an hour. But I ended up phoning you like an idiot after all. They kept saying 'She's out.' So I kept phoning. Then at five—I was sitting in the library studying for Wednesday, and I thought, She'll be coming back to the dorms for dinner. And I ran—right out of the library, all the way back to the dorms. I didn't even wait for the elevator."

"But would you have waited for the elevator if you hadn't been in love?" she asked lightly.

"Oh God!" he groaned. "I know you're not interested."

"But I am interested."

"Susan . . . why don't we just go to the movies?"

They walked down Third Avenue. She had put her arm through his, a young lady on a promenade. They did not attempt to talk, but there were all the antique-shop windows to look at; they stopped methodically in front of each and stared at the accumulations of rickety furniture and ornate china and once useful objects with names that were no longer remembered. Susan hated antiques. It depressed her to think that tea kettles and candlesticks could survive human beings. Her own furniture, she decided, would be as modern and impermanent-looking as possible, and it would fall apart soon after she died. Once, for a moment, she and Jerry were reflected in a massive gold-framed mirror that perhaps had reflected a Louis Fourteenth lady, and Susan saw that they looked like two people who might be walking on together forever, arm in arm, long past the point where Third Avenue ended and there were no more antique shops and the world's unknown space began—they might have looked that way too to the quick glance of a stranger. She let her arm slip from Jerry's, wanting to stand alone. "Are you all right?" he asked.

"Of course." She let him take her hand.

"Maybe we'll find a French movie," he said, "all about the dangers of Paris. People hiding out in sewers."

"I'd love to hide in a sewer."

"You just think you would."

"Maybe I'll do anything I want to."

"Well," he said, "I think you'll be glad to come back here in the end."

She laughed exultantly. "In the end, perhaps. But not in the beginning, not now."

"Oh," he said quietly, "I see."

They had begun to walk very quickly. He was whistling; he whistled "Oh, Susannah" and "Tea for Two." "Hey," she protested, stopping for a moment, "I'm wearing heels." He grabbed her wrist roughly and jerked her along behind him like a disobedient child. She pulled herself free. "I refuse to walk like this, Jerry." But strangely enough, she was not angry with him; she stood before him laughing, feeling an immunity in laughter.

"There's a movie theater four blocks away," he said. "That's where we're going."

"Do you know what's playing?"

"No, I don't. I just want to get there."

"Jerry . . . I don't think we ought to go to the movies." The sound of her voice seemed peculiarly distinct.

"Why not?" he said defiantly.

"I think we should go somewhere and talk."

"Oh," he said slowly, "I know what's coming."

"Do you?"

"Yes, I think I know. You're going to say it's all over—right? That's that." He raised his hand uncertainly, then snapped his fingers in the air. "Is that what you mean?"

He was so permanent, tangible, standing there in the street. It seemed impossible that words could make him vanish. "Yes," she whispered. "I guess . . ."

"Just like that!" he cried.

"Jerry," she said timidly, "it's been coming on."

"Sure. I know." He looked up at the street lamp and then at the cars passing and the people. It seemed to Susan as though everything were moving except them. "This is a hell of a place to have a conversation," he said.

"Better than the subway." She tried to laugh, hoping he would too. She couldn't look at his face.

"Do you feel anything at all?" he asked suddenly. "Do you?"

"What do you mean?"

He moved toward her and put his arms around her, pressing her head against his chest. "I love you, Susan."

His body sheltered her, blotted out the street. She shut her eyes tightly. "I'm sorry," she said. It was all so easy, so swift and antiseptic—dead. She wished she were able to cry. She owed him that much.

"You did love me at the beginning," he said desperately.

But she was somehow unable to remember. When she was a child it had seemed possible to measure love; if you really loved somebody you knew you would weep when they died. She did not know if she would weep for Jerry's death. But that was silly, a child's standard, and yet there were no others. Perhaps she had never loved anyone. She felt his body trembling against hers. Was he crying? "It's not your fault, you know," she whispered. "It's really not."

"Then whose fault is it?" he demanded.

"No one's—I don't know," she said. "It's just the way things are."

"That's easy to say. That's damn polite and philosophical. But it's me! I wasn't enough for you."

"I won't talk about it like this," she said. "I just won't."

"Well, tell the truth," he cried. "Say it was me!"

"Jerry, this doesn't do any good." She hated the words as she said them, but she couldn't think. She wanted to run away, disappear. There was no time to be beautiful. She saw an empty taxi speeding down Third Avenue and just as it was about to pass, found herself waving at it frantically. It stopped. She walked to the door and closed her fingers tightly around the cold metal handle, taking possession. "I'm going back to the dorms," she announced.

"Okay."

"I don't see the point of talking—really."

Jerry said nothing. He strode over to the taxi, yanked the door open and held it for her, "Well," he said, "get in."

"Jerry—look, call me."

"Get in." She climbed obediently into the taxi and slid back on the leather seat. Jerry slammed the door shut. "One hundred sixteenth and Broadway," he said to the driver.

The driver put his hands on the wheel. "Wait!" she cried, turning the handle that opened the window. "Jerry! I want to say good-bye."

He had already begun to walk away. He turned now and stared at her with immense sadness. "You've used me," he said. "I've just realized it."

The taxi sped up Fifth Avenue. She had rolled the windows all the way down, and the wind was whipping her cheeks, blowing her hair into tangles. The stone city was luminous around her, promising, and she was in her taxi in the center of it all—for the time being it was hers.

Later, when she was in her room taking off the black dress, she remembered an afternoon spent with Jerry a year ago, when they had cut classes to go down to the Drive. It had been a Grimm's fairy tale afternoon; there were children looking for berries in the dusty bushes, white pigeons in the sky, and the river was as glassy and still in the sun as if it had been frozen. They had thrown their books down upon the lawn and begun a mock fight, flinging grass at each other, ducking behind trees. "You'll never get away! You'll never get away!" Jerry had mocked her ecstatically. She had let him catch her at last, let him pelt her with leaves and kiss her. Then they had lain beside each other in the grass, smoking cigarettes and talking drowsily as long as there was sun. She remembered now, with a sudden pang, that she had almost wanted to die that way, that afternoon.

CHAPTER FIVE

"I'LL MAKE SOME coffee," Kay said, "once I can find my glasses."

Susan, who had already flung herself down on the awful chintz bedspread, scrambled up hastily. "No!" she protested. "Let me do it! Let me do it, Kay. I know where everything is."

But Kay, ignoring her, went on groping through the litter of the room, her eyes still half blind with sleep. Susan followed her awkwardly, saying, "I can open that," when Kay fumbled with the lid of the coffee jar. "Let me get the cups. I'll plug the hot plate in." She felt a little like a child trailing after her mother in the kitchen, helpless yet wanting to help, to do what grownups did. "I know I shouldn't have come over this early," she apologized shyly.

Kay shrugged and seached the pockets of her bathrobe for cigarettes. "I'm just not quite human yet. I want to take a shower and get some coffee in me. Then we'll talk or whatever."

"Oh, sure," Susan said.

"I was dreaming when you came—a really crazy dream. All about learning that my parents were planning to lock me up in some kind of home for girls—sort of an army camp or prison— and running around trying to find out the rules of the place. You couldn't have sex or telephone calls or read. And there was something about never being able to leave because the place was supposed to be good for you."

"How strange!" Susan said. "I guess you were dreaming about home."

"I wonder what would have happened once I was inside."

Susan was guiltily silent. She had intruded upon Kay's sleep, which had always seemed to her more meaningful than the sleep of other people, interrupted a promising dream, and brought Kay back to a seven-dollar room in the Southwick Arms Hotel at ten o'clock in the morning—all this for her ridiculous need to tell Kay that she had broken up with Jerry. How embarrassingly dramatic she had been, bursting into Kay's room—"Kay! Jerry and I have broken up. It's all over!" And Kay, about to enter the mysteries of her prison, had had to struggle with her bathrobe and say, "Oh God! Just a minute." And then, anxiously, "You're okay, aren't you?" She had not known how close Susan was to giggling at her own absurdity, how little she wanted to talk about Jerry once she had had the excitement of her announcement—what was there to say except that it had been inevitable? She was ashamed that telling was so important, that no act ever seemed complete until it was made public and a little fictitious. She had really come to Kay driven by a restlessness for something new, unknown, something that would begin immediately. Now that she was free, perhaps she could become part of Kay's dark world for just a little while before the ship sailed. Was that being a parasite? she wondered.

"I usually don't have any dreams at all," Susan said. "And they're never like yours. I'm always taking exams I'm not prepared for. Lately I've been dreaming about Mrs. Prosser—isn't that prosaic?"

"Pick up your mail," Kay said. "That's the way to get rid of her. If you want me to, I'll pick it up for you."

"Oh no," Susan said quickly, "I'm going to do it this week."

Kay smiled. "Well, we all have our little hang-ups. At least you manage to get up every morning. It's not a bad deal being a daytime person." She threw a towel over her shoulder. "I'm off to the public baths. How does the corridor smell today?"

"Like cheese," Susan said.

Kay opened the door. "Blue cheese," she said gaily and shut the door behind her.

It was strange to be in the Southwick Arms in the prolonged, conscienceless hotel morning. Susan had always thought of it as a setting for those things that happened only at night: wild parties with beer bottles and jazz crashing into the courtyards, rumored affairs locked behind doors along the green corridors, intense discussions in the community kitchens about whether anything really meant anything—all ending for her, arbitrarily, at one-thirty when the dorms locked up; and so the Southwick Arms had always seemed unreal, theatrical—scenery to be assembled and dismantled at will. Alone in Kay's room, she was suddenly shocked to remember that Kay had actually been living for three months in the real world—for what could be realer than the paint peeling off the radiator? She tried to imagine herself living in Kay's room, although of course her parents would never have allowed it. Yet Kay's parents hadn't allowed it either, just as they hadn't allowed Kay to flip and simply walk out of school in the middle of her last year. It had terrified Susan to see Kay leave college. She remembered wondering how Kay could possibly survive it. "But it's so silly, Kay," she had pleaded. "It's just one more term."

"It's time I learned something," Kay had said, surprisingly calm. "When I've learned something, then I'll go back, when I've stopped being stupid."

"But you're not stupid!"

"I want to see more than fifty per cent when I walk down the street," Kay had said. And Susan had seen her face become luminous. A day later, Kay had moved out of the dorms and into the Southwick Arms Hotel; she had miraculously found a part-time job in the library for twenty-five dollars a week. She began to live on thirty-five-cent hamburger meat, to stay up all night, and to develop secrets—there were usually traces of mysterious visitors around the room: cigarette ashes, half-empty glasses of beer. Kay had even brought her own kind of comfort to the hotel: the books of Blake, Rimbaud propped up on the dresser, and the three prints she had tacked on the wall opposite her bed—a little nun, a pale courtier in a black doublet, and a Japanese girl with a face white as paper—all three austere, fleshless, staring down unmoved upon disorder. Kay's saints, Susan thought.

The morning sun made the green oak leaf wallpaper declare its ugliness; the room looked different at night. Actually, Susan envied Kay this room, even envied her the books she chose to puzzle over—Pound's *Pisan Cantos* was on the floor beside the bed. Susan picked up the book and turned the pages idly, not actually reading; she didn't really like poetry, a curious failing. She wondered if Kay tormented herself with Pound's Chinese inscriptions.

"Isn't the Pound fine?" Kay had come back from her shower.

"I was just looking through it," Susan said, shutting the book.

Kay snatched it up and turned the pages with a disturbing avidity. "Did you read this? Listen—'Pull down thy vanity, I say pull down.' Peter lent it to me."

"It's Peter's?" Susan felt a stir of excitement hearing his name, saying it.

"He brought it over last night," Kay said, smiling tremulously. "He's taken on my education."

Susan remembered that she hadn't told Kay about meeting Peter. Somehow she didn't want her to know. But surely there was nothing wrong about meeting someone accidentally on the street, no reason to feel guilty about it. She wondered whether Peter were in love with Kay and tried to convince herself that would be lovely. "I'd like to borrow the Pound," she said. "Maybe next week."

Kay was staring at her. "You won't be here next week," she said solemnly.

"Oh, that's right!" Susan laughed. "How funny—I never remember."

"But you're going out into the world!"

"Shut up!"

"Miss Susan Levitt, the well-known expatriate," Kay teased. "And she doesn't give it a thought!"

"That's not exactly true, you know," Susan said painfully.

"I know," Kay said. "I guess I'm jealous."

"I wish you were coming with me."

Kay was silent. "I couldn't," she said at last. "Even if I had the money. It's a big thing just to go below 110th Street. I'm too—committed, I guess. No, stuck—that's less elegant."

"You'll finish school next year," Susan said lamely.

"Yes," Kay said, "I'll go back and get my Bachelor's. I think I'll give my diploma to my parents. It's really theirs. Everything's theirs. Even my books. And these pajamas—my mother made them."

They were cotton batiste, white with blue rosebuds and a little lace around the collar—exactly, Susan thought, what a mother would make for a young daughter, someone soft, protected. Kay was furiously picking at the buttons. "I'm not ever going to have children!" she cried. The pajamas dropped on the rug in a little heap. Kay began to pull open all the drawers in her dresser. "Everything's dirty," she groaned. "I can't find anything." It was strange to see Kay without clothes; she was always so well hidden in her dark skirts and shapeless sweaters that it was difficult even to imagine her body. It was terribly round and white, a woman's body, not a girl's. Kay was beautiful, Susan realized. She stared at her in astonishment, until she caught herself staring, and then suddenly Kay's nakedness in the little room and the way she pulled open the dresser drawers as though there was no one there to watch her at all seemed unbearably intimate. For a moment Susan was almost angry with her, not that she was shocked. She walked over to the hot plate and peered down at the boiling water. "Kay, where are the cups?" She didn't want to just sit there on the edge of the bed trying to look unconcerned. It was stupid to be so uncomfortable. After all, Susan thought, Kay wasn't a virgin. Perhaps once you had irrevocably gone to bed with a man, you took your body for granted—you knew, which was different than knowing *about*. She remembered asking Kay once, "What's it really like? How does it feel?" And Kay had only answered, with the maddening smile of an adult, that everything changed too much if you thought about it. Susan still despised herself for having had to ask.

Perhaps she should have gone to bed with Jerry. She had always put it off, telling him, "It's just not the right time yet, Jerry," without ever deciding when the right time would come. And yet she hadn't been afraid. Maybe it was just bitchiness; it would have been different if she had been able to love him—then she could have done it blindly, without questions or after-thoughts. But surely she had loved him a little, at least in the beginning. They had been too shy with each other to think of it then. And now she was graduating a virgin, which was against all her principles. She was sick of being a child, sick of being only a member of the audience. It was time for her to move into the Southwick Arms Hotel.

The pot of boiling water shook in her hand and slopped on the table. "Oh, no!" Susan wailed.

"What's the matter?" Kay asked.

"I don't seem to be able to do anything. Can't even make instant coffee. I wouldn't last a week on a desert island."

Kay laughed. "Most deserts are probably civilized deserts like this with bad plumbing. You'd get along after a while."

"Maybe I wouldn't. I really wish I knew how I'd turn out, Kay, whether I'd survive. I want to test limits. Do you know what I mean?"

"I hear the plumbing's really bad in Paris."

"Oh, Kay! I'm serious."

"You mean you want to go out and look for trouble."

"Yes," Susan said, "even trouble. I think trouble's better than nothing. Kay . . . I just can't stand myself sometimes. Why doesn't anything ever happen to me? Why hasn't anything ever happened to me *here*? I don't even know whether I want to go away. It's just an idea. I just happen to have some tickets. . . . Kay, if you were going you'd *know*, wouldn't you? Things really happen to you."

Without looking at Susan, Kay said, "Well, I've had a pretty strange few months. I'm not sure what it all means yet." She walked over to the table and picked up her cup of coffee. "No . . . that's a lie." Kay sounded as if she were talking to herself. "I do know. I do know."

"Know what, Kay?" She wasn't quite sure that she had any right to ask.

"Well . . . I think I'm going to be a failure," Kay said slowly. "I think that's already settled. And that's all right. But I do want to be a magnificent one. A gigantic smoking ruin. It's the mediocre failures that clog up the world." Kay was staring at her now. "You'll probably stop talking to me, Susan."

"Don't be ridiculous!" Susan cried. "Besides, I don't believe you. I think you're just feeling depressed."

"I'm not depressed today."

"What about Peter?" Susan found herself asking. "Is he a magnificent failure?"

"Peter's very beautiful," Kay said gravely. "But I don't know what'll happen to him."

"But he is a failure." There was a look of pain on Kay's face. "But I didn't mean it that way—I do like him." She smiled at Kay anxiously. "I forgot to tell you—I ran into him yesterday on Broadway. We had coffee."

"I saw you pass," Kay said.

"You should have come with us!"

Kay stirred her coffee. "Oh . . ." she said, "I was feeling anti-social. Anyway, you wouldn't have talked to each other if I'd been there. He told me it was the first time he'd ever had a conversation with you."

"I've been shy with him, I guess."

"That's pointless."

"Kay," Susan asked abruptly, "are you in love with Peter?"

Kay's face reddened. "Really now! Don't I have enough troubles?" She walked quickly over to the dresser, fished out a black sweater and yanked it over her head. "Let's get out of here and look at the morning. I haven't been up this early since I left school."

"Where to?"

Kay was studying herself in the mirror. "Want to walk me over to Peter's?" Her voice was elaborately casual. "I promised to wake him whenever I got up."

"I think I really ought to go back to the dorms, Kay."

"Oh come on, you can just walk me there."

Susan hesitated. "All right," she said.

CHAPTER SIX

THEY DIDN'T TALK at all until they got out of the elevator and heard the music blaring behind Peter's door at the other end of the corridor. "My God!" Kay said then. "He must have left the radio on all night."

"I really can't stay very long," Susan whispered as Kay pressed the buzzer. No one answered. "Maybe he isn't home, Kay. We could go and have some coffee."

But Kay had tried the door. It was unlocked. "He always leaves it this way," she said. She was holding it open, and there was nothing for Susan to do but walk into Peter's living room, where there was no one to listen to the jazz. All the lights were on, though, and underneath the music they could hear the rush of the shower. "Might as well wait," Kay said. She pushed aside a tangle of army blankets on the sofa and sat down. "Looks like someone slept over."

Susan leaned against the door, her hand on the brass knob. The silence between them now was heavy, peculiarly intense, as though anything said would be dishonest. There was no reason for her to wait for Peter—just because they had run into each other on the street, an accident without significance. It would have been a braver thing to have come alone, or not to have come at all, not to have used Kay for this. What was she looking for, anyway? Something to kill time, that was all it was. Amusement. Kay had come to Peter because she meant it.

"What's the matter?" Kay frowned at her. "You look like you're going to take off any minute."

"Oh I'm not," she said tightly, placing herself on a hard little chair near the door. The trespasser's chair, she thought.

Kay had tucked her feet up under her and was smoking a cigarette, staring sad and empty-eyed at an invisible point in an unknown landscape; she might have looked that way sitting alone on her bed in the Southwick Arms Hotel. But maybe Kay's room and Peter's living room and all the other rooms in the world that had been assembled defiantly just for the time being and then neglected, because after all the arrangement was temporary, were rooms in the same endless apartment, connected by miles and miles of dark hallways and worn linoleum, furnished with the massive, imperishable castoffs that parents whose children had left home gave to the Salvation Army. Susan was just a spy, a sneak thief who lived in a room with pink walls in her mother's house.

The rush of the shower had stopped. A door opened, and then there were footsteps coming down the hall. Kay sat up very straight and stubbed out her cigarette. Susan wished she would look at her. "Peter?" Kay called out sharply. "Peter?"

But the black-haired lanky boy in the blue jeans and dingy white shirt who strode into the living room was not Peter after all, but Anthony Leone. "Wow!" he said happily. "Two women and so early in the morning!" Susan began to laugh, feeling giddy, lightheaded. "Hi." Solemnly Anthony nodded to her.

"Hi," she said, trying to choke down her laughter. She had been frightened before when she had thought the footsteps were Peter's; she always laughed when she was frightened.

"These yours?" Kay asked Anthony, pointing to the army blankets.

"Yeah. I'm homeless again. Mitchell finally evicted me."

"Where's Peter?"

"Still sleeping. What did you expect?"

Kay stood up. "I'm going to wake him."

"Oh don't do that. He's in bad shape. We got pretty loaded last night. I got sick, which was stupid."

"Are you feeling better now?" Susan asked.

"Sure," he said cheerfully. "Now I'm hungry."

"I'm going in," Kay said. "He's got his fellowship paper due at five."

"Look—why don't you let Peter sleep. Why are you always so damn motherly?"

"I'm not motherly at all."

"Yes you are. You always have that we-all-have-our-work-to-do attitude. And what's your work, anyway?"

Kay's face went rigid for a moment. "Living," she muttered. "Just living." She marched swiftly past him and up the hall to Peter's bedroom.

Susan heard her shut the door. The jazz was terribly loud. Someone really ought to turn it off, she thought.

Anthony was asking her something: "Do you think she's bugged with me?"

"No," she said, "Kay never really gets angry." But she wondered if that were true.

"What's the matter then? Is she some kind of martyr? I don't dig that at all. I hate passive people!"

"Why?" Since she was alone with him, they might as well have a conversation.

"I hate the way they let themselves be taken in. They're suckers, and suckers are stupid people. God, how I hate stupidity!"

"My!" Susan said. "You're awfully violent."

"Stop flirting with me. I'm serious."

"I've never flirted with you," she said, embarrassed. "I hardly know you."

"Oh no? What about the Riverside Café? We've been flirting for two years now."

There was something attractive about his ferocious determination to be taken seriously. For once she felt older than someone. "You might be right, at that," she said. It was true that for two years Anthony's eyes had signaled to her over all the heads in the Riverside Café, where he was to be found every night standing at the bar until four in the morning, and that she had never been able to resist smiling back at him, even though she knew he grinned appreciatively at all the passing girls. "A campus bum," some of the girls at school had labeled him. But there seemed to be more to him than that. Once when she had been alone in the Riverside, Anthony, drunkenly dodging the little tables in his path, had come over to talk to her. He had told her that he wrote poetry, was a Communist, was only eighteen, and that he had just been expelled from college for bringing a girl up to his room, and could he walk her back to the dorms. She had said, "No. I think I can make it myself." "*C'est la vie*," he had shrugged sadly. "*C'est la vie*." To her surprise, he had walked quickly away from her.

"I saw you with your boy friend last night," Anthony said accusingly, as if there were some dark meaning in having seen them.

"Did you?"

"All dressed up in a black dress, getting on a bus. Did you have a good time?"

"We broke up," Susan said, feeling the words carve themselves at that moment on the walls of the living room. Somehow she had been waiting for a chance to tell Anthony that. Jerry was further away than ever now—history.

"Good!" Anthony cried exuberantly. "Glad to hear it! I think people should break up more often. Did you know that I'm a girl-stealer?"

"Are you really?"

"Yes. Also a parasite. Also a genuine indolent bum. There are terrible stories about me."

"I've heard some," she admitted.

"All true. But someday I'll be a great man. I think society should take care of its artists."

"Oh definitely," Susan agreed gaily.

"Oh definitely," he jeered. "You don't know what you're talking about. You've got rich parents. I suppose you believe in truth and beauty like all the other poopsies."

"I do believe in truth and beauty. Even if it's kind of a cliché, I guess." She couldn't be angry with him; she liked the ridiculous way he flailed the air with his arms when he talked. He looked a little like a windmill, she decided. "What are poopsies?" she asked.

"Sensitive souls who won't drink anything but Italian coffee and talk about Paris being better. There are armies of poopsies at the Museum of Modern Art—all waiting to be picked up."

"What happens to poopsies in Paris?"

"Nothing serious. They get laid a few times."

Susan laughed. "I'm going to Paris."

"You'll get laid too."

"No," she said gravely. "Maybe I'll just walk around and look at things."

He smiled down at her benevolently. "You're a funny chick," he said. Stretching out one of his long arms, he tentatively touched her hair. "You have pretty hair. That's something." His hand lingered on the back of her neck. Susan sat very still. She thought of saying, "Look here, we hardly know each other," but she didn't really mind his hand. Somehow it was no more sinister to be touched by Anthony than to be touched by a child. What would it be like if Peter ever touched her? The jazz sounded like the way he walked, the shambling, uneven steps, the forward thrust of his head. She made herself think of Kay and Peter talking to each other now in the warm, blind-drawn dimness of the bedroom, the closed door shutting them in together—that was the way it should be. They even looked a bit alike with their heavy heads, and their voices had the same feverish quietness. It would really be beautiful for them if they loved each other. There were amazingly few people in the world that you could love. Maybe she would find someone in Paris. . . . Anthony would call that "getting laid" and maybe that was all it would be for her, a gratuitous act of sex—those words at least had a kind of scholarly dignity. She supposed that after all she was a poopsie, but she'd die rather than admit it. Anthony's face was moving closer and closer to hers—she could almost feel the warmth of his breath. Hastily, she stood up and walked to the window.

"Susan!" she heard him say reproachfully, "I was going to kiss you."

"Oh it's too early in the morning," she said.

"No excuse." She was silent. Standing at the window with her back to him, she watched the janitor five flights below sweep the courtyard. Anthony hadn't moved. He was probably staring gloomily at her back. It was a little disappointing. She was almost waiting for him to walk across the room. She wondered whether he was shy. After all, he was only eighteen, a little boy, a waif. When she turned away from the window, he was sitting on the sofa, bending over a book. "What are you reading?" she asked in a voice she recognized as the too interested voice grownups used with children.

He did not look up. "*Prison Etiquette*," he muttered grudgingly.

"Oh, what's that?" she said. She felt loathsome, utterly dishonest. It was all a game—she didn't know what she wanted.

"A book about C.O.'s—Conscientious Objectors, to you—how to get along in prison."

"Are you planning to go to prison?"

"They might take me away," he said. "I've had this book out six months from the library, and now I don't even have an address for those postcards they bug you with."

She sat down beside him. "I can never return library books either. Once I had to pay an eight-dollar fine."

"Yeah? That was pretty dumb." Suddenly he smiled at her. "You're weird," he said with evident satisfaction. "You're another one."

"Another what?" she asked anxiously.

"One of the club. I'm a freeloader. Peter wants to do himself in, preferably in the Packard. And you—you won't let anyone touch you. That's your particular little kick."

"That's not true!" Susan protested.

"Oh, I don't care." He yawned elaborately. "All I want is my breakfast. How are you fixed for money?"

"You'd better get a job if you want money." Her face was hot with anger.

"I knew you'd come out with some bourgeois moral thing like that," he said triumphantly. "Christ, I knew it the minute I saw you. I'm always running into girls like you. That's my fate. I bet I'll never meet a really great woman. Just little nowhere girls all my life until I marry one." He stalked restlessly up and down the room. "I wish Peter would get up so I could have some breakfast. I wish they'd stop screwing in the bedroom. That's really too much!"

She tried to think slowly, carefully, to be calm. All of a sudden there were hundreds of little wheels spinning inside of her, as though Anthony's words had set a machine in motion. She remembered the proud, shy way Kay had said, "Peter's taken on my education." If it was true that Kay went to bed with people, of course she'd go to bed with Peter. But Kay hadn't told her, and she had always assumed that Kay told her everything. The wheels were turning much too fast. She wanted to get out of the apartment immediately. She didn't want to look up the hall to the bedroom. And she didn't want to care. "I think I'm going," she said to Anthony. "Tell Kay I'll see her." She got up and walked to the door.

"Now you're angry," Anthony said sadly.

She shook her head. "No . . ."

"Oh look, don't go. Christ, that's so silly."

"I just—want to, that's all. Besides, we weren't getting along very well."

He had stood up now. "I really do think you're very pretty," he said.

"Thank you."

"And it's really true that I'm hungry. All I had yesterday was a frankfurter."

She looked at his face and saw for the first time how white it was, how dark and huge his eyes were. There were two buttons missing from his shirt. "I can lend you a dollar." She felt embarrassingly overfed.

"Well gee . . . fifty cents would be fine. I don't know when I can pay you back."

"That's all right."

"Why don't I go down with you now? I'll have breakfast and talk to you. And you'll have coffee. . . . Okay?"

Why not? she thought, why not? She knew she didn't want to be alone.

"Okay," she said.

CHAPTER SEVEN

ANTHONY WAS TWO years younger than she was, but a lot had happened to him. Only two years before, he had been a senior in a parochial high school in Pittsburgh. Something had boiled up in him that last year, a delinquency of books and violence. "I hadn't read anything till then," he told Susan. "*Ivanhoe*, Dickens, *Popular Mechanics* and the Bible—nothing! I played basketball." Somehow he began to stumble across other books—Thomas Wolfe, Rimbaud, Huxley, D. H. Lawrence. "I read some of *Ulysses* and thought Joyce was nutty. And of course I was reading a lot of crap too." He wrote two notebooks of poetry and hid them in his locker. At the same time, he was terribly bored; he found himself provoking fights all the time and not even knowing why. In one of his classes he announced dramatically that he would no longer go to chapel because he could not believe in "the myth of God." He was expelled. His father had beaten him. "Just because he believes that people should be beaten," Anthony said, suddenly furious. "He didn't care. He never went to school, that hypocritical old bastard." His fists clenched; he eyed all the people in Schulte's as if he were looking for someone to hit.

"Okay," Susan laughed. "It's all right."

"He said he'd get me a job in the steel mill. Big deal! That's where I'd end up if I went home now. I said the hell with that. Then the school said they'd take me back if I promised to go to chapel—I was a good student or something. So I went back. There's an anticlimax! But I decided to have a good time. I went to town on some of the papers I wrote, almost caused a couple of riots. But anyway they gave me honors in a lot of crap when I graduated, and I got the scholarship I just bitched up. . . . By that time I was completely cynical."

"Are you still completely cynical?" Susan teased him.

"Yeah." He grinned.

"What's your poetry about?"

"About? I don't know—whatever hits me. It's good. Listen—I wrote this one a week ago. . . . " He recited the poem too rapidly, as if he wanted to say all of it at once.

Somehow she could not really hear it. Perhaps it was good. Sitting in Schulte's with Anthony, she could not take her eyes off the street. And yet it was funny, she thought—if she had been outside at that moment, she would have been staring in, at the tables, the people, probably at Anthony; so in a way you never ended up seeing the place where you really were at all, not that there was much to look at in Schulte's. The same paper roses had been on the tables ever since she was a freshman; the same people continued to come even though the coffee was awful. Kay was always there. She said she only felt at home in nondescript places, so they usually ended up in Schulte's on the long, shapeless afternoons when they had both cut classes. Kay had taught her what a significant and necessary thing it was to cut a class, not just an irresponsible act. Her parents, paying bills for "advantages we never had," would not understand, but stolen time had such a liveness to it; you could really feel yourself exist, knowing that the barrage of facts was continuing six blocks away without you. How long it had taken her to discover this! Peter, Kay and Anthony must have always cut classes. They were outlaws, part of a mysterious underground brotherhood. How was it that she had suddenly become able to recognize them, thinking, There's one, there's another, the recognition instant and uncanny. "Screwed-up people," Jerry called them, seeing them all as casualties, those who would never "make it." "What's wrong with Kay?" he would ask. "Why doesn't she wear lipstick, go back to school?" "I don't know," Susan had answered, embarrassed because he made her feel that something should be done about Kay: "Listen, Kay, it's such a simple thing to put on lipstick." But for Kay it couldn't be simple. Sometimes she thought Kay was like one of those captains who went down with their ships, although it was hard to believe in that sort of thing.

It was strange that Anthony had called her "another one." But of course she did have a bad reputation. Probably very few people thought she was still a virgin. No one knew how much she lied, how skillful she had become in making adjustments in reality: inferences, suggestions, a few dark strokes, a laugh she had learned from someone. A shy Southern girl in the dorms had once said wistfully, "Susan, sometimes you're so-o-o bizarre." Disgusting! She would have to stop lying in Paris. A fresh start, a clean break—she had begun to think like a criminal. It was bad enough to be a coward. It was all upside down for her too; most people were afraid of reputation, not of the acts themselves. It was stupid to ruin your reputation and have nothing to show for it. You didn't even have the comfort of being defined as an outlaw—that was something to be, one of a community. Instead, she had always been a scrubbed, prissy little girl who ate all her cereal, who sat scared stiff with her hands folded while another little girl poured red ink on the floor "just to see what would happen" or said "I don't care" to the teacher. It was easier to be good. But she had always secretly watched the wild girls, wanting to be one of them, never daring: eighth-grade Marjorie who had flunked history with a total lack of concern and had tagged after all the cigarette-smoking boys in high school; and now there was Kay. She had brought Anthony where Kay would have brought him, almost automatically. "Let's go to Schulte's," she had said. "I like that place."

"I don't know why. It's no place at all."

"That's why I like it." They had both laughed—a moment of rapport. Later it might be harder to be Kay. If she spent the day with Anthony and he asked her to go to bed with him, Susan would have to say that he had misunderstood, or didn't he see that it would all be so meaningless? She had always liked the word "meaningless"—it was something you said after everything happened to you, when you no longer cared about caring or not caring. It was a graceful way out, a regretful smile over a glass of champagne. "But it would all be so meaningless." She would flourish that above her emptiness until it fitted her. And Kay would give love and never mention it and perhaps go bankrupt— putting her to shame as she listened outside the bedroom.

*　　*　　*

"Let's go soon," Anthony said. She nodded. Half an hour before, he had said, "Let's split," and she had said "Soon" and ordered another cup of coffee, somehow reluctant to leave, afraid of missing something.

Now she saw a man and a girl turn the corner two blocks away and begin to walk down Broadway, the girl shapeless in a black sweater, lagging a bit behind the man, whose walk had a peculiar uneven rhythm. He looked straight ahead, never back at the girl, who now and then caught up with him. She could not see their faces. It was difficult at first to tell that they were together. Susan watched them through the window coming closer and closer.

A block away. There was still time to put down her cup, say, "Okay, let's go," pay the check, walk out and rescue the afternoon. Now Anthony was talking about taking her to the Frick Museum. "The Met's too big. I go out of my mind there. There I am digging a Rembrandt and I'm thinking about the Japanese paintings I haven't seen yet and the whole goddamn Greek wing, and I feel like running because I haven't got time, because in two hours they're going to close up the place." Susan nodded absently, watching the two figures in the street. "But you don't understand. For most of my life I didn't see anything, anything at all. Then— New York. Wow! Too much." Anthony shook his head sadly. "Too much. Hey, stop looking out the window!"

"There's Kay and Peter," she said. She had been waiting for them all along. But it was only to see them, to see the fact of them together.

"Where? Listen, let's leave anyway. I want to talk to you."

"I just want to see Kay a minute." She was beginning to feel completely treacherous.

"Yeah. A minute," Anthony jeered.

They were crossing the street. Anthony stood up and waved to them through the glass. They saw him and waved back. It seemed to her that she had planned everything, even the waving.

"Spies! Spies!" Anthony hooted as they came into Schulte's. Everyone was laughing. She laughed too. She saw now that Peter and Kay had the same faces they always had. You couldn't tell that they had made love to each other. Kay smiled at her in a rather embarrassed way and seemed to be trying to whisper something about being sorry. "Listen," Peter was saying, "the system is inescapable. You might ask us to sit down."

"Breakfast or lunch, Peter?" said Anthony.

"You son of a bitch! I'll just have coffee. Have to get back to work. That's what Kay says, anyway."

"Have something to eat—some eggs," Kay said softly.

"But I never have eggs. I exist mainly on the Chinese dinner and the kindness of friends." He paused as if he expected them to laugh, but the words had been too elaborate. The odd thing was that what he said was probably true. Susan wondered why she liked him. "Why do you always try to feed me, Kay?"

"It's an old Jewish custom," Kay muttered.

"But it's much more sinister than that. Kay wants to fatten me up so that I'll make my contribution to mankind. You should always walk behind me too, Kay, with a little bell, so that I won't waste any more of my time. Do I have fifteen minutes left to have my coffee and get back to the apartment?" Kay was silent. "Maybe I won't go back at all."

"Oh, you'll go back," she said.

"Do you think you'll get the fellowship, Peter?" Anthony asked.

"I might stand a good chance, if I had more time to fill out the application."

"There's enough time," Kay said.

"Five o'clock—three hours."

"Well, hurry up, man. Come on. Someone get the waitress." Anthony stood up.

"God!" Peter said. "If I could only get out of New York, out of that hole I'm in. You can get good cheap apartments at Harvard. I'd throw everything out, buy new furniture . . ."

"You should give a big party before you go," said Anthony. "With a jazz band."

"Yes. A final disaster!" Peter agreed excitedly. "Will you come?" He spoke suddenly to Susan, forcing her to look at him.

"I'll be in Paris," she said. He was sitting next to her and had stretched his arm along the back of the booth. An arm in a blue shirt sleeve. She resented it fiercely.

"Come to my party. Don't go to Paris. Conditions are bad all over."

"Is it any different at Harvard?"

"That's very good," Peter said. "It's too bad you're always so quiet."

"I'm just well brought up." She wished he'd stop looking at her.

"She's a poopsie," said Anthony. "But I'm going to reform her. I'm going to make her wild and strange."

"And what will you do with her then?" Peter asked. He put his hand on her shoulder—anyone might have done that, she thought. Kay was frowning darkly over the menu.

"I'll make love to her. Listen, she's nice. She bought me breakfast."

"I don't like to be talked about," Susan protested.

"No?" said Peter. "I think you love it."

"It's really very dull," she said helplessly.

"But you *do* love it."

"I wonder where the waitress is," Kay said, carefully propping the menu between the salt and pepper shakers. She gave Susan and Peter a sad, dazed stare.

"Kay," Susan said, "Anthony and I are going to the Frick Museum."

"You'll see my nun there."

"Why don't you come with us?" Susan felt as if she were talking to a stranger.

Kay shook her head. "I like to be alone when I go to a museum."

"What do you do when you're alone?" Peter demanded. "What are your secrets, Kay?"

"I won't tell you my secrets," she said quietly.

"That's right," said Anthony. "Don't tell Peter anything."

Peter laughed harshly. "You are all against me."

"That's not true!" Kay cried. "That's not true!" She almost stood up, as if she wanted to rush over to him and protect him from everything with the softness of her body, but she didn't even touch his hand. Everyone was silent. Peter drummed absently on the table.

The waitress came and said, "What'll it be?"

"Coffee! Coffee!" Peter sounded as if he were invoking a deity. Kay's face was impenetrable again.

"Peter," Susan said coldly, "why must you know people's secrets?" It was true that they were all against him, she thought. He was the enemy, with his reckless, disinterested probing.

Peter didn't answer her at first. He picked up a spoon and weighed it in the palm of his hand. "Because I have none of my own," he said finally. For a moment she doubted him, but he wasn't performing now; she almost wished he were. "I even keep a record of my dreams," he added. "Typewritten. Very impressive. That's my one great project. When I die, I'll bequeath it to the university."

"Is that true?"

"Yes," he said. "It's true. Five black folders. You're terribly curious, aren't you? Would you like to see them?"

"No," she said, retreating uncomfortably, "I wouldn't."

"Why not?"

"Well . . . I just think that dreams should be private."

"What else do you think, Susan?" Peter asked relentlessly.

"What do you mean?"

"What do you think about me, for example?"

She began to feel frightened, as if at any minute she were going to find herself standing naked in front of him, yet she wanted him to go on, wanted the pain of it.

"The way you stare when you're not talking is very mysterious. What are you looking at? Are you seeing everything? Digging everything? Or do you see nothing at all?"

"Sometimes . . . nothing," she whispered, her face burning.

"Well, Susan, I got very drunk last night and called you. Kay knows."

Kay was a white blur across the table. Susan had to force herself to speak. "I'm glad I wasn't in."

Peter laughed too quickly.

"Say, Susan, we should go to the museum," Anthony said.

"I'll drive you downtown," said Peter.

Anthony seemed puzzled. "Oh, we can get there. . . . And you have that fellowship thing. . . . "

"It's late, Peter!" Kay cried.

"I can't get it done. It has to be in at five. There wouldn't even be time to type it."

"I'll type it for you," Kay said wearily. "I won't go to work."

"I don't want any favors, Kay. I can't get it done. I can't just sit down and write it carelessly now."

"You've got three hours, Peter. You could try."

"I'll try again in the fall," he said brusquely. "It comes up again in the fall." He got up from the table and turned to Anthony. "Come on," he said. "I'll drive you. Maybe we'll all just go for a drive and have a beer somewhere. It's a good day for that."

"Well . . . all right," Anthony said dubiously. "You'll come?" he asked Susan.

Susan avoided Peter's eyes. She knew if she said she wouldn't come, he might go back to his apartment, he might even fill out the application. They were all waiting for her to answer.

It was a good day for a drive, she thought. Broadway was full of sun and cars and racing children. She wanted to be set in motion too, to run mindlessly and not feel too much. She couldn't do what Kay would have done. She was herself. She wanted to be saved from boredom even for a few hours. "I guess I'll come," she said.

"Let's go and find the car," Peter said to Anthony.

She watched them go up Broadway. A sprinkler truck groaned by, spraying the streets, and she saw them step back on the sidewalk a moment too late to escape the wave of wet mist. Peter wiped his face. It seemed very funny. "Peter got wet," she said to Kay. When she looked out of the window again, she had lost them. "I wonder if he remembers where he parked the car. He seems terribly inefficient." Kay still had said nothing. "You're coming with us, Kay, aren't you?"

"I have to go to work."

"Oh . . . I always forget that you're not in school." She watched Kay stub out her cigarette and take another one from the pack. "What's the matter, Kay? What's happened?" she asked, even though she knew, they both knew. Kay's face was blank. "I mean, are you angry with me?"

"Angry? No. I'm not angry." Kay's dark eyes narrowed, trying to focus. "I think I will go on the drive," she said abruptly. "I don't feel much like working. Sometimes it's like being buried alive surrounded by all those books. It's stupid, though—I need the money." Her face was very tired, as if she knew too much. Perhaps she would look that way all the time when she was forty. "I've had a hundred afternoons like this," she said. "No one doing anything—me, Anthony . . . I knew Peter wouldn't try for the fellowship, you know."

"Kay!" Susan cried. "Do you think I use people?" She had been rehearsing those words for a long time. "Jerry said so last night. Do *you* think I do?"

"We all use each other," Kay said.

"But I did use Jerry."

"And Jerry used you. Everybody uses everybody. That's the way it is." Kay's voice was flat.

"But there has to be more than that, doesn't there? There has to be love. Maybe I've never really loved anyone." Her confession terrified her. She had only half thought of it before, had never meant to say it.

"I think you're worried about words," Kay said. There was no absolution.

"But I don't want to go on using people!"

"It's just the way you look at it," Kay said.

CHAPTER EIGHT

IN AN ODD WAY, Peter's car was the place where he really lived—he only inhabited his apartment. It was true that, like most of the things Peter owned, the ramshackle black Packard should have been allowed to die quietly ten years ago, but a curious desperate joy possessed Peter at the wheel as long as everything went fast, and he always kept the back seat littered with the fragmentary preparations for a journey: blankets, an old raincoat, books, aspirins, a box of crackers, can openers, socks—as though the chaos of his living room had simply been extended. Peter didn't seem to care that the car shook every time it hit a bump and that its insides were ticking so loudly that everything had to be shouted. "This car is going to shake itself to pieces one of these days!" he called out cheerfully.

"Why don't you get it checked?" Anthony asked.

"Because I'd find out too much was wrong with it. I'd never be able to bail it out again."

They were all in his power that afternoon; he had made the car their only reality. "Sing," he'd command them, and they'd sing. No unfinished work existed in their world. He was golden and they were golden. They drank a lot of beer. Is it because of the beer? Susan wondered. Even Kay was smiling. She sang all the choruses low-voiced, but anyway she sang. They drove twice through Central Park, then all the way down to the Battery, passing gray office buildings, processions of gray people down avenues—"You're too serious!" Anthony shouted at them through the window. By four o'clock, they were uptown again, passing 116th Street, the red buildings of the college somewhere behind the apartment houses. "Are we going to New Jersey?" Susan asked, but she knew it didn't matter. They had destroyed logic three hours ago, made the afternoon their midnight. "I'm drunk!" she laughed, letting her head fall against Anthony's shoulder. "I'm so drunk. I feel like everything is twenty miles away."

Anthony kissed her. "Am I twenty miles away?"

"Oh . . . maybe fifteen." She liked having him kiss her. It was all part of the ride. Everything fitted. "You smell of soap," she said, "like a little boy."

"How come you know so much about little boys?"

"None of your business."

"Susan, why don't you adopt me?" Anthony said. "I'm young, I'm hungry, I'm broke, I'm miserable. We'd have a ball."

"I can't adopt anyone," she said, enjoying the game. "I'm going to Paris in a week."

"We'd have a whole week," he said.

"No. I have too much ironing to do." She expected him to laugh, but he only looked unhappy. It occurred to her that he might be serious.

"Oh, adopt him!" Peter had turned around to look at them. "Why don't you adopt him? Just walk hand in hand into the Southwick Arms Hotel, have breakfast in Bickford's. It would be awfully good experience, Susan."

Her anger surprised her. "Why don't you watch the road!" she cried.

"Perhaps I should." With an infuriating smile, Peter turned away again.

They left the West Side Highway and began to drive through Washington Heights, through endless streets of blond brick apartment houses and stores with names like "Foam Rubber City" and "Food-O-Thon" and women wheeling baby carriages home from the supermarkets. Edgecombe Avenue, Fort Washington Avenue—"There are too goddamn many avenues here," Peter said. "Too goddamn many living rooms. You be a good girl, Susan, and they might let you live up here. You could have a living room with wall-to-wall carpeting and a dishwashing machine."

"I don't want to be a good girl!"

"Too bad. That's your particular fate."

Peter was looking for a way to get down to a little dirt road he remembered that ran by the river—there was a mad Puerto Rican bar there, he told them, and a dilapidated yacht club. Once he had found the road by accident and looked at the water all night. "It's the greatest place in New York, if we can just get there." But all the streets led back to the highway. He began to drive too fast; the car was shaking and ticking. Kay sat rigid in the front seat, clutching her pocketbook. "It's getting late," she said.

"It's four-thirty," Peter said icily. "Why is that late?" He was forcing the car up a hill. "Why doesn't someone sing, '*In the evening, by the moonlight, you can hear the darkies singing . . .* '? Kay, how does that one go?"

"I don't like that song."

"I knew you wouldn't sing it." He laughed and put one arm around her. "Kay, Kay . . . don't be dull. Don't be a self-conscious liberal."

"I am what I am," Kay said sadly.

"Christ! If I thought that, I'd kill myself." The car screeched around a corner.

"Peter! Don't!" Kay cried.

"Wow—take it easy, man!" said Anthony.

"What's the matter with all of you? Don't you want to fly? It's the slow people who have accidents—you should know that. You want to fly, Susan, don't you?"

"I don't want to get killed," she said, but she almost shouted "Drive faster!" She wanted to ride in the front seat with Peter into night and emptiness, to a place where all the clocks had stopped and no one cared. She would sing for him if he asked her to. . . .

Anthony had moved close to her again. Now he reached out and took her hand, which became an object, something someone else was holding. "We both have dirty hands," he whispered. She pretended not to hear him. She was tired of the game. Maybe she would never say "Drive faster" to anyone, but only the frightened words she didn't mean. But it must be beautiful to fly, even if it killed you. "Peter!" she called out desperately, "Peter!"

"Do you want me to slow down?" he said. "All right, I'll slow down."

"No . . . I just—wondered where we were." She couldn't quite remember now what it was she had wanted to say, and she would drown if she thought about it. She laughed helplessly and leaned back against Anthony's arm. "Peter, perhaps I will adopt Anthony," she said brightly, trying to pick up the lost pieces of the game—it was safer, safer.

"Yes, go ahead—adopt him," said Peter. "Every young girl should adopt someone."

"Shall I take you on?" she asked Anthony.

"If you do, you'll have to sleep with me."

"But I've never slept with anyone."

"No!" he said incredulously. "Well, I think you should start."

"Oh I agree." The game was spinning itself out thinner and thinner. "Do you think I should, Peter?"

"Do whatever you want," he said with an odd impatience. "I give no advice." Kay had turned a locked, mute face to her.

Suddenly she thought, Why not? Why not? "Yes," she said. "Okay, Anthony. I'll meet you tomorrow."

"What about immediately!" he cried, acting his part. "This afternoon! Now! Now!"

"All right," she said. The car had stopped for a red light. She opened the door and got out.

"Susan! Where are you going?" How funny it was that Anthony was still playing the game—if she got back into the car again nothing would be changed; she would simply have made a rather elaborate joke. Peter and Kay were staring.

"Let's go downtown." Even then Anthony didn't believe her. No one believed her.

"The light's going to change," Peter said very patiently.

"Aren't you coming downtown, Anthony?" She walked carefully to the sidewalk. Everything was racing now. The air was full of eyes. She stood on the curb and waited for something to happen.

"Listen! Just a minute!" Anthony was scrambling out of the car at last. He leaned through the rolled-down window and whispered something to Peter, who nodded, his face expressionless. Then she saw Peter hand Anthony something—a key. They seemed very businesslike, almost formal. But why didn't Peter cry out, "Susan, don't go! What are you doing!" although she might have known he wouldn't do that—perhaps not even if he cared. Kay would be alone with him now; they might even find the road by the river. Susan smiled at her, wishing that Kay wouldn't look so concerned; you could tell she was thinking, "Susan's flipping." That made it all so dreary, and this was her moment. She had never had a moment.

The car started forward as soon as the light turned green. Anthony stepped toward her, tall and solemn. "Shall we take the IRT?" he asked awkwardly.

"Fine." She hooked her arm through his and they began the march to the subway. I'm doing it, she thought. I'm doing it. I'm doing it.

For a long time she thought she heard the car just behind them, the machine-gun tick of its innards. Once she looked back, which was silly, because she knew the car had gone in the opposite direction.

CHAPTER NINE

"I DIDN'T THINK you'd do it," Anthony said.

"What?"

"Come back with me, I mean."

"I said I would." Susan laughed. For half an hour everything had made her laugh.

"I kept thinking you'd escape in the subway."

"I almost did."

"You're mad," Anthony said approvingly.

"All right. I'll leave right now." She brushed a lock of hair off her forehead and began to walk sedately, heels clicking, down the hall, but that was only part of the game. She felt fine, like someone in a movie.

Anthony grabbed her wrist at exactly the right moment. "Sure. Go on. Leave." They smiled at each other; then they both looked at Peter's door, which they hadn't opened yet. "I'll find the key," Anthony whispered. He was still holding her hand, as if he didn't quite know what to do with it. She realized they had been standing in the hallway for a long time, whispering at each other like two children about to do something dangerous. He opened the door and then stepped back and waited for a moment as if he were reluctant to go in, but at last she followed him into the courtyard dreariness of the apartment. "I'll turn on a light," he said.

"Not the overhead light! I hate that."

"Okay. The lamp." He walked to the door, which she had left standing open, shut it, and she heard him fumbling with the chain and for the first time felt frightened.

"Oh don't lock it!" she cried.

"What's the matter?"

"It's locked already."

"Okay." He stared at her, puzzled, a little sad. She kicked off her shoes and crossed her legs under her on the couch, trying to look comfortable. "Can I have a cigarette?"

"Here." He was still watching her. There seemed to be nothing to talk about. "You shouldn't smoke," he said finally. "You don't inhale—that's a waste."

"Sometimes I want to smoke."

He came and sat next to her and took the cigarette away and put his arms tightly around her. "Let's go into the bedroom," he whispered.

"Not yet."

"Come on." She felt his lips against her neck.

"No. Please, not yet."

"All right. Do you want to talk? You talk—I can't." He sat on the arm of the couch. "I keep thinking about laying you!" he cried joyously. "I've been looking at you for about two years. You were always with some hopeless guy. Today I thought you were after Peter—he was turning you on."

"I'm not after Peter," she said angrily.

"Look, I don't care! We're here—that's the crazy thing. Don't you understand anything? We're here."

She got up from the couch and walked aimlessly across the room to the bookcase. She had never looked at Peter's books before.

"What's wrong?" Anthony said.

"Nothing."

"Are you afraid?"

She shook her head.

"I won't hurt you."

"I know."

"Just maybe a little."

"I know all that. I know everything. I had Modern Living when I was a freshman."

"That's very, very good," he said sarcastically. "Jesus Christ! Don't say things like that!"

"Why not?"

"Oh, come off it. Why do you want to sound like a dried-up old woman? I've seen the alumnae from your school with their suits and their hair screwed behind their ears. Why do you have to sound like you're so tough? I know you've never been laid. I think that's great. I don't care if you talk like a virgin. I know you're scared."

"I'm not scared," she snapped.

"Well, you should be."

"That would please you?" He did not say anything at all. Her words hung in the air until a moment too late she realized they were from the wrong movie; she had not meant to sound that way. Anthony was turning on the radio—a blur of stations, the news, Campbell Soup, "*I'm all shook up/Oh, I'm all shook up.*" Shaken up, she thought facetiously. *Shaken* up. *Shaken* up. The song fell apart. "It's too loud, Anthony," she said.

"It's a loud song."

"What's he all shook up about, I wonder?"

Anthony shrugged.

"Don't you know?"

"Maybe you should listen to the radio now and then. You can't read Virginia Woolf all the time."

"I don't especially like Virginia Woolf."

"Shall we have a literary discussion?" Anthony said bitterly. He got up, grabbed the nearest book and walked out of the room. She heard the bedroom door slam. The radio was really much too loud. She couldn't think. She considered turning it off. Her hair was a mess and her lipstick was all gone, no doubt, but she had left her pocketbook on the table near the door. She couldn't reach it. She wondered if she were expected to leave now, or was Anthony lying on the bed waiting for her to come in, listening for the sound of her footsteps in the hall, the opening of the door he had shut. But Anthony didn't know she couldn't move. Susan imagined Peter and Kay coming back hours later and finding her still sitting paralyzed on the couch. They would ask her what was wrong, and she would say, "Nothing," and they would all go out for coffee at Schulte's—they might even go for another ride.

After one more song, she thought, I'll stand up. And she concentrated fiercely on the impossible act of standing and managed to uncurl her legs, and stood. Either I'll go in or I won't. But no one just stood in the middle of a room—that was more embarrassing than sitting—so she walked up the hall.

When she rapped on the door, there was no answer. "Anthony . . . Anthony . . . " He was playing his part too, she decided. She pushed the door open, said, "Hi," and sat down quite calmly beside him on the bed. To her surprise, everything had become automatic again. He was smoking a cigarette and staring up at the ceiling.

"I thought you'd gone," he said after a long while. "Are you going back to the dorms now?"

"I don't know."

"I think you should."

"Anthony . . . can't we talk?" she asked uncertainly.

"I don't want to talk. I don't have anything to say."

"Please don't be angry."

"I'm not angry with you." He sat up now and looked at her. "I think you have a lot of guts for a girl—up to a certain point. And that's all right."

"I don't have any guts at all," she said, feeling a terrible sadness and an anger with herself for telling him this. "I just do things sometimes, and don't even know why. That's not having guts."

"I don't know," Anthony said slowly. She had wanted him to say, "Yes, it is. Yes, it is." Why else would you tell anyone something like that about yourself? She wanted to fix her eyes on his until she saw her concealed image in them, but he had turned away as if he were embarrassed.

Anthony slid off the bed and stretched his arms. "Christ! You'd think it was the middle of the night in here!" He walked over to the window and pulled up the blinds. Suddenly the glare of late afternoon was in the room. Shadows raced across the ceiling.

In another apartment, someone was practicing a Clementi sonatina, picking it apart, each note separate, wavering. "I used to play that when I was a kid," Susan said, wanting desperately for a moment to be the little girl she had once been, but somewhere the continuity of her past had broken. The little girl was a stranger now, almost a fiction—once upon a time there was a little girl named Susan who practiced the piano. Now there was a different Susan who was stretching herself out on a bed, deliberately, without conviction, without love or whatever it was one was supposed to feel. Her body had never seemed so long; the sheet was terribly far away.

Anthony was standing over her. "Come on. Get up. Don't you know it's dangerous to lie around on beds?"

"Just a minute." She began to laugh because it was all inevitable, all decided now, and he didn't know it. The outlaws were about to welcome another member.

"Come on. I'll walk you back to the dorms."

"But I'm lazy."

He stared down at her, absurdly serious. "You can get up. Give me your hand."

"Here." She extended a limp wrist to him. Anthony sat down beside her.

"What are you doing, Susan?" he whispered. She felt herself smile at him, and then she reached up and touched his hair, which was strangely soft, like a child's. He seized her hand and held it away from him, squeezing her fingers together until they hurt.

"Don't do anything you don't mean!" he cried.

"How do you know what I mean?"

"I don't get you at all," he said painfully. "Maybe you're just a bitch."

She said, "Maybe," just to say something, because what was said didn't really matter. She felt nothing but an immense curiosity about what was going to happen next. She stared in wonder at the walls of the little room—it seemed as though at any moment they would spring shut like a trap and she and Anthony would be buried in darkness—but Anthony didn't necessarily have to be there at all; it wouldn't make any difference who was with her.

"Okay," Anthony said. "Okay." And she felt the bed shake a little when he got up. Then the blinds were drawn down, and she knew he was standing in the corner by the window, taking off his clothes. In the darkness she could barely see the walls of the room; they hadn't shut her in after all, but had fallen away, dropping her into the middle of a vast, unknown space. "It's so dark," she said.

"Susan . . ." She felt Anthony's body press against hers.

"Wait," she whispered. Sitting on the edge of the bed, she began to undress. "Clothes are terribly complicated, aren't they?"

"Yeah," he said shyly. He was watching her, of course—her back prickled with the knowledge of his eyes and she was slower than she need have been—it seemed as though he might have asked permission. When she lay beside him again, his hands were impersonal, tracing invisible lines on her body, measuring her, not touching. How odd to be naked with a stranger! She wished he were someone she had known all her life with all the suspense between the two of them of never having known how the other really looked. Instead it had been very easy, something that could be done lightly. It's like people at the beach, she thought, with a tightness in her throat that made her think she was going to laugh.

There was not even much pain—a vague feeling of something inside her, moving. This was what going to bed with a man must be like. She could hear everything very well: the bed, his breathing, the tick of the alarm clock on the bureau. His body drove at hers over and over again. Her legs were cramped. She hadn't thought it would take so long. She would have to tell him he was too heavy, complain that the sheets were wet—she didn't want to lie between them any more—now she remembered that they had been Peter's and Kay's first. But she had always assumed that the sheets would be clean. She wondered if the used sheets made the experience what her mother would call "sordid."

"Anthony . . ."

"I love you," he whispered. "Don't talk."

All at once, when she despaired of it ever being over, he cried out, almost as if he were in pain. Perhaps something had gone wrong. She felt him shuddering against her and he sounded as if he were crying. Not knowing what else to do, she put her arms around him. He was terribly thin. She could feel all his bones, the sharp, delicate skeleton of a bird. It was embarrassing. She had always imagined a rape, an overwhelming of herself, the victim, never that she would be left with a starved, spent child and the guilty sense of her own heaviness. "Are you all right?" she asked helplessly.

CHAPTER TEN

HE HAD SO many plans. He was going to show her things she had never seen before, reveal the city to her. "Have you ever seen shipyards at night? Have you ever seen white steam coming out of smokestacks with the sky pitch dark? It's terrific! Tomorrow night we'll go to the Brooklyn Navy Yard!" he shouted. "I'll borrow Peter's car." Water was rushing into the sink in Peter's kitchen, and Anthony was clattering cups and saucers around in it, delighting in the noise he made. He didn't seem to notice her silence. "We'll go back and forth on the Staten Island Ferry and eat hot dogs. Would you like that?"

"I've been on the Staten Island Ferry," she said.

"Not with me!"

She wanted to be alone—alone with her body and her emptiness and the unchanged face she had seen in the bathroom mirror. He had insisted on making coffee and she didn't want coffee. There was something terrible about having coffee with him now, about watching him move around the kitchen as if their bodies had never even touched, and yet she still smelled like him. If something happened, why didn't it really happen? Instead she was being promised smokestacks and ferry rides as if she were a child. Where was the moment when everything became luminous and the earth shook? She would remember being bored and not knowing what time it was.

"It's late," she said, not wanting to speak at all, but in a little while she was going to say she had to leave and she didn't want her voice to fail her. She was going to sound pleasant and ordinary. Why wasn't it possible just to leave in silence?

"It's only nine. We've got hours, baby." His arms swooped down in front of her, put cups on the table, saucers, spoons. His sleeve kept grazing her cheek. She stood up.

"I'm in your way," she said.

He stared at her uncertainly for a moment, then smiled. "You're not in my way."

She wished she hadn't gotten up—it was too soon—how silly to have to sit down again. "Well . . . all right," she said, subsiding awkwardly into the chair.

He was still looking at her. "You're pretty," he said with an unnerving eagerness. "I like you best without lipstick."

"I don't."

"That's because you're hung-up on being elegant. You like to put on that black dress and have some guy take you downtown and buy you cocktails. Right?"

"Sometimes," she shrugged, for some reason feeling a little ashamed, almost wanting to tell him that the black dress frightened her, that she had never quite lived up to it. But he was laughing now.

"Oh yes, sometimes!" he joyfully mimicked her. "Listen—we'll do that. That would be terrific. But you'll have to pay—I haven't any bread at all. I'll pay for all the ferry rides."

She found herself laughing too. "I don't love you, you know," she said in desperation, "I don't love anybody."

"Jesus!" he cried. "Who said anything about love?"

"No one."

"I don't love you. You don't love me. Right?"

"Right!" Susan said emphatically, but it had somehow become impossible to be honest with him even if she told him the truth.

"But—we like each other?" He sat down opposite her and put his feet on the rung of her chair. "You're strange," he said, as if he were pleased, as if someone had given him a strange little animal to hold in his hands.

"Strange?" She felt a frightened giddiness.

"You like to make everything a little complicated. There's nothing complicated about the Staten Island Ferry."

"Well . . ." she said, "I'm going away in five days, that's all," believing that less than ever.

"So we'll have five days." He began to wind a lock of her hair around his fingers. "Let's not be sad now."

"But I have things to do."

"What things?" he asked indignantly.

"Oh, shopping, seeing people. All kinds of class meetings."

"That's shit," he said. "You don't have to do all that."

"Yes, I do."

"You'll go to the Staten Island Ferry," he said a little belligerently. She didn't answer. He unwound her hair and let it go.

"If I were going to be around for more than a week you'd get pretty sick of me," she said, trying to laugh. "You like to know lots of girls. You like to sit in that bar and talk to everybody and get drunk and say '*C'est la vie.*'"

"That's only because I'm not with you."

"No, you like it. Really. That's the way you see yourself."

"I see myself with you this week," he said sadly. "I see us talking and wandering. I see us making love. Then, okay—so you go. It's not so complicated."

"I don't know," she said.

"Listen, when I first came to this city, I used to walk everywhere—miles! Just walk and look. I wanted to live in Chinatown."

"It's late," she said again.

She couldn't quite look at his eyes, but she saw him moisten his lips with his tongue. "I want to be in my room," she said. How odd that sounded, but why should it be odd to wish to be in one's room? "I want to be alone." Too loud, she thought immediately. It came out wrong, false, but she was somehow committed to it.

He had gotten up, was standing at the stove watching the water boil.

"I'm sorry . . . I'm tired, I guess."

"Sure," he said, grimly cheerful, "alone, alone. Greta Garbo has to be alone. Pour some instant in the cups, will you?"

"I don't think I want any." But he took the pot off the stove and brought it to the table and stood silently waiting for her to open the jar and measure out two tablespoons of coffee. "It's too warm for coffee." Susan felt as if she were going to suffocate. "I'm sorry . . ."

"Don't be sorry."

"Okay."

"Look—" he began. She looked at the pot which he still held and began to giggle guiltily. He banged the pot down on the table. "Listen to me!" He grabbed her by the shoulders. "Next time it'll be better. Next time I'll make you come!"

"Your hands are wet!" she cried shrilly.

After a moment, he removed them from her shoulders and with a white, desperate smile began to dry them on his shirt.

"I really do want to leave," she said, trembling. She made herself stand up.

Anthony strode over to the refrigerator. "We'll have iced coffee," he said, jerking violently at the ice tray. "It's not too warm for that."

"Anthony, listen . . . I . . . " He began to pound the ice with his fists. "Oh stop! Please . . . " She plucked at his sleeve and was shaken off like a kitten. "Anthony, it's not your fault!"

"Thanks!"

"It had nothing to do with you. It was an experiment." She had an astonished moment of triumph—she had never been more honest with anyone. "It was an experiment," she repeated, "that's all." Everything in the kitchen was rattling. He seemed to be trying to pull the refrigerator down. Suddenly the ice tray came loose in Anthony's hands. He turned slowly and confronted

Susan holding it. There was blood running down his fingers—his eyes accused her.

It was horribly quiet in the kitchen. She tried to think of something to say, but one sentence after another shattered inside her. "I don't want any coffee," she said.

"Why don't you go, then!" he yelled. "What are you hanging around for?"

"I . . . I just wanted . . ." But she couldn't remember ever wanting anything.

"Why don't you *go!*" He flung up his arm and blindly hurled the ice tray away from him, across the room.

There was the sound of glass breaking, falling, splintering all over the floor—then silence until someone shouted down the black tube of the courtyard, "Hey! What's going on down there!" and she saw the smashed pane in the kitchen window, the jagged wound in the glass that had not been there a moment ago. Was the window really broken? But if you thought about things like that, you would begin to fall—slowly, as if you had been dropped out of an airplane in a nightmare. It was strange, too, that the night was a slightly different color where there wasn't any glass, and strange the way Anthony kept looking down at his bleeding hands and then at the window as if it were the window that had hurt him.

"Wow!" he whispered, strangling the word. Was he afraid she would find him ridiculous for talking to himself? Should she offer to help him sweep up the glass, say, "Don't worry about it"—what was expected of her? She remembered the softness of his hair suddenly, the way he had clutched her when they had been in bed, and felt a peculiar hollow ache in her armpits. There was so much loneliness about the way he stood, all alone in the middle of the kitchen, not even angry but as vacant as she was, watching the ice cubes melt on the floor.

She wanted to put her arms around Anthony, let him close his eyes, but he might not understand. He might push her away or begin to kiss her—that would be frightening, humiliating. She folded her arms and pressed them against her body as if she were cold. She would think about it. There was still a little time— Anthony hadn't moved.

The doorbell rang, unreal in the silence, rang again. Without even a final look at her, Anthony rushed out of the room. But how could he go when she had almost decided to touch him? Now he was opening a door, shouting to someone. "I'll pay for everything!" Then the door slammed and she thought she heard him running down the hall to the elevator. There was someone moving around in the living room, but it wasn't Anthony—he was gone. Her arms still folded, Susan confronted only the kitchen's emptiness, the little square of linoleum where Anthony had stood.

"Susan?" She looked up and saw Peter standing in the door-way. "Hello," he said uncertainly.

"The window's broken," she said after a long while.

He walked into the kitchen and looked at the window with-out saying anything, peered down at the glass on the floor. Then his eyes were on her again. "Are you all right?" he asked, half as if he cared, half as if he were just curious.

"Yes," she whispered, "but the window . . ." He was standing exactly where Anthony had stood. A painful lump was forming in her throat.

"Sit down," Peter said. "Come on."

"Oh, I'm really all right."

"Sit." Peter dragged a chair across the kitchen floor and gently pushed her down on it. He took off his jacket, tossed it into her lap, and knelt down to pick up the glass.

"I'll help you."

"Just sit there." Methodically, one by one, he was picking up the splinters and dropping them into the garbage can. He placed the ice tray carefully on the kitchen table.

"Anthony threw it—but it was my fault."

Kneeling among the pieces of glass, Peter had an odd, secret smile. "Well, it let some air in." He stood up and walked to the window and thrust his arm through the hole in the pane. "It's a very respectable broken window." The way he said that reminded her of the careless way he crossed streets, the way he drove his car.

"You don't care." Her arms had slipped into her lap. She stared down at them wearily, a little surprised.

"Not particularly," she heard him say. "It's almost summer."

For a moment she felt a funny abstract hatred for him. "Why don't you break your own windows?"

"Why don't you cry?" Peter asked quietly. His face had collapsed into sadness now that he had stopped smiling.

"I don't know." The lump in her throat was swelling larger and larger.

"Just cry—you're going to anyway."

"I don't want to." A bitter fluid had begun to run down her cheeks. If she cried, she would cry forever. "I don't want to," she wept, "I don't want to."

CHAPTER ELEVEN

SHE DIDN'T WANT to think. The mornings were the worst times. For three mornings she woke up much earlier than she wanted to; the first morning it wasn't even six. She would lie stunned on her bed, afraid to move, and it would only be for the moment of waking that she would not remember anything. The early light in her room would be white and sunless, and the room itself would not be quite familiar to her; it would look as though its space had been subtly altered during the night, as though the objects in it had lost their color, grown larger.

She would not be able to go to sleep again, so she would tell herself that in only two hours it would be time for breakfast and that she could, if she wanted to, get up now and turn on her lamp and even take a shower and put on the dress she was going to wear that day—except that there would still be the problem of what to do before breakfast.

But already she would have begun to remember. Already the scene in Peter's kitchen would be playing itself over and over again, she weeping while Peter watched, the evidence of details accumulating—the color of Peter's shirt, the four beer bottles on the window sill, the coldness of her fingertips when she had pressed them against her eyes. After a while Susan could see it all with such heightened clarity that she would no longer know how much she remembered, how much she imagined.

I ought to get up, she would think—there was no comfort in the damp, twisted sheets of her bed—but her body would be as strengthless and limp as if it had spent the night wrestling a fever. She would not be able to recall what she had dreamed. Better not to know. Better to stop thinking before one knew too much. There was something about Peter that forced too much knowledge upon her. He was as dangerous, as compassionless as a mirror. She would not see him again before she went away. At first she told herself that it was for Kay's sake, but she knew very well that that was not the reason.

When she was leaving that night, he had followed her down the hall to the door. For a moment they had stood facing each other, and she had known that he was holding her there, forcing a dizzying closeness upon her as powerfully as if he had thrust his body against hers. "I'll see you," he had said to her, not in the casual way that people often said that, but somehow stating a fact. And she had felt—even remembering it she felt—as much joy as terror. She wished it had not been said at all.

The afternoons were easier for her. It was easy to find ways of not being alone. She gave herself up to the college. If Peter called, she would tell him how busy she was now before graduation. The first day she was measured for her gown, and then there was the Class Sing and a speech by the Dean; the second day there was the Class Luncheon. The third day there would be the graduation rehearsal; the fourth, the graduation itself; the fifth, her departure.

Peter didn't call, of course. She knew that he wouldn't; he would wait for her to find him. But she had no time to walk up and down Broadway looking for faces.

Sometimes it amused her that with hardly any effort she could be such a convincing senior. Maybe all that was needed was sheer physical presence and a bland face. Strangers never looked at you hard enough to see that you were sleepwalking. When she went to the Class Sing, only someone listening to her with particular interest would have noticed how few of the songs she knew, that she sang only disjointed fragments of the lyrics, like "youth's happy shore will evermore . . ." and something about lifting one's glass on high "*sans souci.*" It had only been a week ago that she had sat in Kay's room and said, "I'm not going to bother to go to anything. I wouldn't even go to graduation if it wasn't for my parents."

She was glad that Kay hadn't called either. Kay would have made her feel guilty, ashamed, as if she were betraying her as much by going to the Class Sing, the Class Luncheon, as by liking Peter too well.

She found a window on the top floor of the dorms from which she could see all of Broadway. First, the two blocks nearest the college where nothing ever happened, then 113th, 112th in miniature, a reduced Schulte's and Riverside Café and the anonymous figures that skittered in and out of them and could have been anybody. If you had a photograph, she thought, the photograph would contain everything really—not only the people you glimpsed in the streets, but people you couldn't see, people containing invisible thoughts behind walls and other windows. You could have the photograph and look at it forever and know that it contained everything, and it wouldn't be enough. But at least a photograph asked nothing of you, would never watch you cry.

On the day before graduation rehearsal, Susan had just come from the Luncheon, was just crossing the campus on the way to her room, when Mrs. Prosser, the postmistress, suddenly materialized on the same brick path.

Susan felt perfectly calm in a stunned sort of way. It even occurred to her that ironically enough this was the first time she had ever known that Mrs. Prosser was definitely not on duty.

"Miss Levitt," Mrs. Prosser said, "you still haven't picked up your mail."

She had nothing to say, no excuse. "I know," she said. "I'll pick it up."

"I've never heard of such a thing—a girl not wanting her mail."

"I know, Mrs. Prosser," she said politely.

"Well, you come with me now and get it."

"No . . . I'll get it later." Maybe I will get it later, he thought.

But then, without warning, Mrs. Prosser gave her a sudden shrewd, terrible look, as if she knew the most intimate things about her, as if Susan stood before her wearing only her secret dirty underwear. "You're a very peculiar girl, aren't you?" she said in a soft, shocked voice. She turned from Susan without further comment and took up her slow, elderly journey across the campus.

"You're a very peculiar girl." She was standing on the path exactly where Mrs. Prosser had left her and the words were spinning around and around, shaping themselves into a judgment. She was peculiar. Her terror of Mrs. Prosser was peculiar, her fear of getting her mail. She wouldn't be able to get it now until she had graduated, until she was immune and could stride laughing to the mail desk—"You see, Mrs. Prosser, I've come to get my mail"—as if it were a joke they shared. The letters would be dead by then, and meaningless. She could throw them away unread if she wanted to. But would she ever be immune? Her fear was peculiar. She was peculiar.

She made herself walk the rest of the way to the dorms, made herself climb the stairs, walk down the hall to her room. In her room, she would be temporarily safe.

There was a note on her door. From Mrs. Prosser, she thought, barely surprised. But it was from Kay:

Susan, where are you?

CHAPTER TWELVE

ACROSS THE LAWN, in the gymnasium, someone was counting to three over the loudspeaker: "One . . . two . . . three . . . one . . . two . . . three . . ." The numbers boomed and died in the air. She was being counted off and subtracted.

The graduation rehearsal had begun half an hour ago, but she found herself incapable of hurrying to it. Slowly she walked across the deserted lawn in her high heels, since no one was watching. If it hadn't been for the voice, you might have thought that the college was closed for the summer, the gates locked to all except the janitors. She felt a great weariness, as if some machinery inside her had finally run down.

They had changed the gymnasium, made it unfamiliar. She saw a long, uneven line of girls standing frozen in procession, with rows of empty wooden chairs for an audience. A little stage had been built too, and the Class President, whom Susan identified as the voice over the loud-speaker, was standing precariously at the edge of it, shouting: "Girls! Please make *sure* you're in alphabetical order. I want everybody to turn around and memorize the face of the person in front of them and the person in back of them." Susan wondered if everyone was actually going to do this—it seemed a terrible indignity. But at least it didn't apply to her.

How dressed up everyone was, adult, already vaguely secretarial. She was dressed for the occasion, too, in a dress she had never worn before because it had too many little buttons on it; someday she would get around to cutting them off with a razor. Her mother said the buttons "made" the dress. Perhaps she would give the buttons to her mother, who was really the person she had dressed for today. They had all dressed for their mothers because tomorrow they were going out into the world to perpetuate them. Why rehearse? Why graduate? Why make it public that you couldn't even cut the buttons off your dress?

"Aren't you going to get on line?" A girl, dimly remembered as the Class Secretary, had approached her.

Susan thought of possible rebellious answers. "Well, where are the L's?" she asked, although she knew that if she looked she would find them immediately.

"Just line up alphabetically," said the Class Secretary, in what was obviously her most reassuring voice.

"Thank you," said Susan. "Thank you." Walking to the L's, she was on the verge of laughter. She remembered with a slight malicious thrill that she was peculiar.

The loud-speaker was crackling ominously—they were going to have trouble with it. Just like a girl's school to have trouble with the apparatus. The rehearsal was going to be interminable. One more day to go now, Susan remembered with a sudden panic.

The Class President announced that now that everyone was present, she was going to call the roll. She opened the roll book, then examined her pencil point. "Abbott," she read loudly. "Abrams." She bit off each name and annihilated it with her pencil, scarcely waiting for the anxious little cries of "Here! Here!" There was something appalling about such efficiency, but maybe it would take only half an hour to call the roll. "Allen." "Here!" "Armour." There were still three hundred other names. The afternoon was shrinking. *Susan, where are you?* She was locked in the gymnasium and couldn't get out. Not that it mattered—she would probably just go back to the dorms later, anyway; she would have another night of too much sleep.

In the middle of the B's the loud-speaker uttered a piercing shriek and died. "Oh dear," the Class President said. "One . . . two . . . three . . . one . . . two . . . three . . . Testing!" she cried boldly, jabbing the microphone with the tip of her index finger. "Can you hear me?" she called to the girls.

"No!" everyone shouted cheerfully. They were all laughing as if a holiday had been declared. They were still only schoolgirls. Susan liked them for that, but their laughter was making the rehearsal longer. The Class Secretary had gone for the janitor, and now he was entering the gym, crossing it in slow motion. He was peering at the amplifier and fiddling with some wires. Hurry! It was two o'clock on Broadway—Kay was sneaking a forbidden cigarette in the stacks of the library; Peter, who had probably gotten out of bed an hour ago, was just about to go out for coffee. . . . Nothing was happening at all. And everything was happening and happening without her. She felt time leaving her as if it were being bled from her body.

The loud-speaker was fixed at last. They finished the B's, eliminated the C's, the D's. When the Class President reached the G's, Susan found herself listening for Kay's name. "Gorman," she secretly prompted, "say Gorman." "Gordon," said the Class President. Kay would have been called next, but they had taken her name off the roll months ago. "Grant," said the Class President without hesitation, as if Kay had never existed.

When her own name wasn't called, Susan wasn't surprised.

Of course, she thought, almost relieved. She stepped out of line and began to walk across the endless gymnasium, names falling weightlessly around her like dead leaves. Words. Sounds. How strange to be named anything. If you weren't on a list, you had no name—you weren't even absent. Well, head up anyway. Back straight. In a gymnasium you had to remember your posture even if you were peculiar. She was walking to Paris. No—Broadway. No—she was going to get her mail.

Dear Miss Levitt:

Due to lack of attendance, I regret to say you will not receive credit for Physical Education VIII. As you know, the completion of the Physical Education program is a degree requirement. Therefore you will not be eligible for a degree this spring.

Please stop by my office this week. I am sure you will want to make up this credit over the summer in order to obtain your degree in the fall, and we will be able to arrange a sum-

mer program for you at one of the colleges in the city. My office hours are 4:00 to 5:00 P.M. Monday, Wednesday, and Friday.

> *Sincerely,*
> *Ethel Stroheim*
> *Physical Education Dept.*

The letter was two weeks old. There was something familiar about it. It was a letter she had received often in dreams.

Standing in front of the mail room, Susan read it several times. It was difficult to concentrate. Mrs. Prosser watched her from her little window, but it didn't matter; she had lost her power now. Susan stuffed the letter into her pocketbook with all the others and went back to the gymnasium.

"Excuse me," Susan said loudly, placing herself directly in front of the Class President, who had been chatting with another girl, "but I'm not graduating this May, and I wonder where I'm supposed to stand or if I'm supposed to stand anywhere. My last name is Levitt."

The Class President and the girl exchanged looks. "Just a minute," the Class President said distantly. "I have to get the roll book." Returning with the book open to the last page, she announced, "Here you are. With the October graduates."

How strange that it had already been written down. "Who are they?" Susan asked, her voice even louder.

The Class President frowned and explained rapidly that there were eleven October graduates, that they lined up behind the

May graduates and stayed in their seats when the diplomas were being handed out.

"Thank you," said Susan. "I wasn't quite sure."

"They're sitting in the last row now," said the Class President. "Oh really?"

But she couldn't quite walk to the last row yet. She stood for a while in the doorway of the gymnasium, as if she were someone merely passing by who had paused there and might walk away at any moment. She was looking on with interest, with nothing more than interest.

There was a girl in a tight blue dress on the platform now, droning a speech to the rows of vacant, listening faces. "Our unforgettable years . . ." said the loud-speaker, ". . . and the Alumnae Association . . . I urge you to join . . . we wish to thank . . . our last class meeting . . ." The audience awoke and applauded.

The girl on the platform produced a large white box. When she opened it, a piece of white tissue paper drifted to the floor. "Next there'll be rabbits," Susan thought, struggling to make herself laugh. But the box was full of orchids. Sunlight had suddenly filled the gymnasium and all the girls were applauding again. For some reason, her hands were clapping too. The wooden floor turned golden and dust glittered in the air. Strange, she could almost smell these orchids—although orchids had no scent. Two weeks ago they had asked each member of the Senior Class to contribute a quarter—"For orchids" they had said—she had never paid her quarter. When she remembered that, she stopped clapping. Luckily her dress had pockets; she hid her hands and tried to become just a person standing in the doorway again.

There were twenty girls whom everyone was supposed to be grateful to. One by one, as their names were called, they rose from their seats and came to the platform to receive one of the orchids she hadn't paid for. In a moment it would all become ridiculous— twenty orchids pinned crookedly on twenty bosoms. "The orchid is an obscene flower," Kay had said once. Why couldn't she laugh? Why had everything become so unbearably significant?—these pastel girls with the sunlight falling on them coming to get their orchids, their perfect, pleased children's smiles, the engagement rings protecting them. It was miraculous that they existed. The other pastel girls who had been lazier, a little more indifferent, who watched now and applauded, were also miraculous. They too would always graduate; they would be safe. Not me, she thought. She was the one who couldn't clap, the odd one. Not me. At last the pain of it was alive inside her. Not me. Not me.

CHAPTER THIRTEEN

THE SOUTHWICK ARMS Hotel was much too quiet, too much a hotel of the imagination. Today the corridors had a deathly smell of disinfectant and all the locked doors with their shiny brown paint looked exactly alike, as if the rooms behind them were exactly alike, too. A pile of tangled, grayish sheets lay at the end of each corridor; it must have been the day they changed the linen. Kay once had said: "They change the linen once a week and that's how the inmates mark time." Only today there didn't seem to be any inmates. Perhaps they had all turned off their lights, their hot plates, and fled, leaving behind them only their castoff sheets and here and there a container of milk on a window sill. Perhaps as always she had arrived a little too late.

But all the way down Broadway she had had the oddest feeling that when she walked into the Southwick Arms Hotel this time, she wouldn't ever leave; it would really be possible to rent a little room there, find some sort of job—better than going blindly, meaninglessly to Paris. Instead she could enter the Outlaws' world, Kay's world, but now hers—she had qualified for it, graduated into it, she thought bitterly. Maybe everything was even part of the same plan—the graduation rehearsal, the predestined walk to the Southwick Arms Hotel because Kay wasn't in the library. That was a comforting idea. But the hotel should not have been strange today, it should have been the way it always was. Why had they turned off all the radios?

There was a thin bar of light under Kay's door, but Kay didn't answer. Susan knocked again. At the library they had said that Kay was sick. If she was sick, wouldn't she be in her room? Susan put her hand on the doorknob and listened, straining to catch the first stir of Kay getting up from her bed, her chair. "Kay," she called softly.

It was absolutely silent in the corridor. "Kay!" She almost hated Kay for not being in, for writing, *Susan, where are you?* and sticking it on her door, summoning her here and now having absconded with the answer. "Kay!" One couldn't keep calling to an empty room. In a moment she would have to go.

But then there was a cry from Kay's room. "Who is it?"

She found that she hesitated before she answered, allowing herself a second in which she could have walked away. "Susan."

"Susan?"

"Yes."

The door was opened. Kay had the mute, fierce look of someone who had been caught hiding.

"Were you asleep?" Susan asked lamely. Kay was staring at her as if she were a stranger.

"Come in." As soon as Susan had stepped into her room, Kay closed the door, forcing it shut with the weight of her body.

"I thought they'd come for their rent," she said with a choked laugh.

"Do they do that?" It was the sort of stupid question she always asked when she didn't know what to say. It meant, "Yes, I heard you," implied a concern she often didn't feel, an innocence she'd never had. Part of her style—Susan recognized it now for the first time and realized that it had just become obsolete.

"Yes. If you don't pay." Kay attempted another laugh.

"Is something wrong? Are you sick?" She felt as if she were inquiring about a third person whom neither of them knew.

"Am I supposed to be sick?"

"According to the library . . ."

"Well, I'm sick of the library. Are you going to stay? Why don't you sit down?" Kay swept a pile of books and tangled underwear off the armchair. It was odd that Kay was offering her the chair—usually they both sat on the bed cross-legged. "You're all dressed up," Kay said.

"I hate this dress."

"It looks good on you." Kay sat on the edge of the bed, a cigarette in her mouth, striking one match after another. A silence was settling upon them.

"You put a note on my door," Susan said.

"You didn't call."

She had the uncomfortable feeling that Kay was reproaching her. "I was going to but then I didn't. I went to sleep." Kay was frowning absently at her unlit cigarette. "Today I went to the graduation rehearsal."

"Oh yes," said Kay. "The graduation scene." Her voice shook a little. "That's why you dressed up." She spoke as if she were pronouncing Susan guilty of that.

"Kay!" Susan cried. "I'm not graduating. I flunked gym." The fact instantly lost its meaning, became something else—an appeal, something that had once belonged to her that she was trading in for compassion.

"Oh . . . I'm sorry," Kay said hastily, as if she hadn't quite been listening.

"Well," Susan said, "it doesn't really matter." But that was what Kay should have said.

Now Kay was looking at her. "You're bugged about it." Her voice was curiously flat. "Let them keep their piece of paper," Kay said. "That's all it is, you know, a piece of paper."

"I know," Susan said. I'll go soon, she thought.

Kay got up and walked restlessly around the room. Her hair was uncombed; she kept touching it, pushing it back from her face. "Their rules!" she cried out suddenly. "Their idiot rules!" She turned and faced Susan, her eyes alive again, feverish. "You didn't even want to go to graduation—now you won't have to. You know how I was going to spend tomorrow afternoon? I was going to get drunk, all by myself. But now we'll get drunk together. In the Riverside Café. We'll have our own celebration. We won't have to sit through the Dean's speeches."

This was what she had come here for—to hear Kay tell her that they were upside down together, out of it together; to consider the peculiar institution of graduation, put it in its proper perspective, strip it of its importance. "You know," Kay said, triumphant now, "it's right that you're not graduating. It has a kind of symbolic beauty."

But I want to graduate, Susan thought. Yes, that was what she wanted. She wanted to march in the procession, wanted the cap and gown, her parents smiling in the audience. "I want to graduate, Kay," she said, not daring to look at her.

"But you have graduated! Does it matter what they put on their records? You can't be ashamed of flunking something like gym that you shouldn't have to take at all."

"But they didn't do it to me!" Everything was suddenly very clear; there was something she could no longer pretend not to know. "I did it to myself. I cut gym. I knew the rules, and I cut because—"

"Because you didn't care! Because you didn't give a damn!" How easily Kay finished the sentence for her.

"But that's not the way it was for me." She wondered sadly whether she was going to lose Kay now. "*You* would have decided not to care."

"Yes, I hated college, the whole idea of college—listening sheep!"

"But that's a way of caring. You hated it and so you were really there and knew what it was and felt it. Well, in a way, I never went to college at all. I was just putting in time at a place that was school, because I'd always gone to school. And I was afraid of it ending, I guess. I'm afraid of going to Paris, you know that?"

"Nothing will happen to you in Paris. You can take good care of yourself."

"But I don't want to go on taking care of myself. I want to let things happen to me, Kay. I thought today . . . I thought maybe I won't go to Paris. I might even take a room in this hotel. I thought of you, the way you lived. . . . " She stopped; Kay was laughing bitterly.

"Oh, Susan, don't make me out to be some kind of—heroine. That's really a drag, you know. It is! Look." She began to rummage through the books and papers strewn on the bed. "Here—look at this. . . ." She hurled a small sketch pad at Susan; it landed at her feet. Susan stared down at it before she picked it up. She wondered whether Kay really wanted her to see it. "Go on. Look."

Even then, she opened it reluctantly, afraid that Kay would expect her to say something she wouldn't be able to. The pad was almost half filled. There were little drawings in it of objects— a chair, a bottle, a lamp—the same things drawn over and over again, darkened and blurred by erasures, their shapes timidly outlined with the same faint pencil, as if Kay were really drawing their disappearance. The sketches made her sad. She didn't know what to say. She turned the pages as slowly as she could. When she looked up, she saw that Kay was crouched over a book. "When did you do these?" Susan said at last.

"I did the last three today." Kay hardly lifted her head. "That's why I didn't go to the library."

"Oh."

"Pretty stupid," Kay said harshly.

"No . . . " Susan faltered. "I just didn't know you were interested in drawing."

Kay's face reddened. "I'm not. I'm interested in—seeing."

"In seeing?"

"Oh hell!" Kay sighed wearily.

"But what is it you want to see, Kay?" One more day, she remembered again. It was already five o'clock and she and Kay were shouting to each other across space, like people on long-distance phone calls shouting uselessly, "Can you hear me? Can you hear me?"

"Just chairs and things," Kay said. "Just chairs."

"But what does that mean? I don't know what you mean."

Kay retreated into silence, arms folded, her mouth taut. "I mean chairs," she said at last, "that's all. This room"—she gestured awkwardly—"this is my reality. This is the big soup I'm in . . . I've got to see it!"

"But you see so much! I've always envied you."

"Envied me! I don't see poems. I don't see paintings. I don't see people. I don't see you. But I'm beginning to see chairs. That's pretty good. Like that one—that's a very important chair. It's where I sit most of the time. So I've been making drawings of it."

"Yes, I saw . . ."

"Well, doesn't the last one . . . ?" Kay began eagerly. "Well, it looks like it a little—I think. I was very happy when I did that." She stopped and looked hard at Susan. Susan opened the pad again. "You don't have to look for it. They're all bad drawings. Forget it!" she cried out. "I don't want you to look at it!"

Slowly, Susan put the pad face down on the table. "I never think about things like that," she said carefully, "about 'seeing'—I mean, not in the same way."

Kay had picked the pad up from the table; now she closed it and set it down again. "You don't think about things like that because"—she hesitated—"because you're not a Mediocre. Oh, I've decided, by the way, that I'm a Mediocre. That's a good word for it." She gave the "o" in Mediocre a hollow, French pronunciation. "I thought I was going to turn out to be something else. But if you are a Mediocre, you're lucky if you can find it out as soon as possible. It's not knowing that fucks everything up."

She had never heard Kay sound so sure of anything before. It was frightening, like someone very old staring at a white wall. "I don't understand," she said sadly. "I wish I knew how to argue with you."

"That's right, you never argue."

"But I think you're wrong. I do. I . . ." It was strange to hear herself objecting, when, yes, she did understand. Wasn't she perhaps also a Mediocre? "Kay," she asked, "why did you leave that note for me yesterday?"

Kay wasn't looking at her any more. "Because I was alone and I couldn't stand it." Her voice was so low that Susan could barely hear her. "This is a bad time of year, everyone going away, graduating . . . you graduating, especially. I got to feeling sorry for myself. I had a really big, disgusting self-pity day planned for tomorrow."

Susan felt an odd disappointment. She couldn't quite accept the unfamiliar real Kay who had written *Susan, where are you?* simply because she had needed her. But what could she have said to Kay yesterday? What could she say to her now?

"I never thought you'd be getting drunk with me," Kay said with a tight little smile. "You will get drunk tomorrow, too—won't you, Susan? What time will you come over?"

"What time?" She remembered that she never liked the Riverside Café much in the afternoon. There was something disturbing about sitting in the darkness of one of those green leather booths when you could see through the plate-glass window that outside the sun was shining on Broadway. And there were never enough people—only those few who were always there, like the derelict old man who incessantly cracked his knuckles. Tomorrow, though, there would be a lot of people on Broadway walking past the window to the graduation. "What time?" Why was Kay pressing her, why did they have to make arrangements? She would sleep late tomorrow morning; she would have called her parents by then, would call them tonight, in fact. How strange to be able to think of something that hadn't happened yet as something already in the past—another form of cowardice!

"What's the matter?" Kay's voice deafened her. She didn't want to answer, couldn't answer. "You lave a look on your face."

"Just a look," she said.

"You were thinking about graduation."

Can't I do that? she thought with a guilty anger. "Kay, I wish we could go to another bar—even a bar in another part of the city. You know what I mean?" Kay's face went rigid, silent. "It's going to be weird sitting in the Riverside. I don't think I—"

"You'd rather not meet, then."

"No, I didn't mean that." Helplessly, she felt the end of the sentence slip away from her. Other words, half formed, impossible to say, crowded her throat. She did know what she meant— that was the trouble. There was no way not to be cruel now, no way at all. "Kay," she said slowly, "I could march tomorrow, if wanted to, with the October graduates."

"Is that what you're going to do?" Kay spoke with cold precision, settling it for her somehow.

With a slight shock she heard herself say, "I think so." Kay said nothing. "I just feel I have to. Isn't that stupid?"

Kay walked across the room, away from her, and sat down on the bed. "Well, I know why you're doing it."

She had a wild hope for a moment that perhaps Kay did know—she didn't quite understand it herself.

"You're making a sacrificial offering to your parents."

The words rang in her ears a long time. This was the end of something, the end of the Southwick Arms Hotel, the end of Kay—another line drawn across her life. "I'm doing it for myself," she said, and wondered sadly whether Kay heard her.

CHAPTER FOURTEEN

THERE WERE TOO many people embracing in the lobby and then too many people on the lawn, too many mothers in little white hats, and the girls were all standing in their black gowns, in the sun, blinking, having pictures taken—"Smile," their fathers were saying, "smile," and they all smiled very well. "Excuse me," said Susan, grimly pushing her way through the crowd. She was looking for her parents—they hadn't waited for her in the lobby. It was difficult to look for people you didn't want to find. You ran the risk of not seeing them, and yet everybody became them for a moment. She began to feel the panic of a child lost in a department store. Her gown was too long: people kept congratulating her because she was wearing it and she kept tripping over the hem. Perhaps she'd tear it, confront her parents in black rags, clearly an outcast. She was tired already of the conversation they were going to have now that they hadn't had last night, sickened by the apologies she was going to have to make, the explanations that would not be quite the truth. You had to protect your parents; you always had to lie a little and each time you lied a little piece of you was eaten away. And you lied to protect yourself, too. They had a way of rushing in upon you if you ever let them think they knew what you were feeling. You had to protect yourself from their greed. They wanted all your secrets; they wanted terrible scenes where everyone wept and forgave one another. At the same time, they wanted you to preserve their innocence. They wanted that most of all.

She had left Kay's room the night before and gone straight to a drugstore to call them. It had seemed so possible at that moment to finally reveal herself to them, to tell them everything. But there weren't any empty phone booths, and by the time she got to the next drugstore, she had somehow done too much thinking. She had sat in the booth, listening to the phone ringing twenty miles away in her parents' house. It rang a long time and she had remembered that they would be just sitting down to dinner. She had imagined her mother coming in as usual to set the glasses of tomato juice on the table, her father putting down his newspaper to draw the blinds, the two of them sealed up inside their house in their bedroom slippers and their well-worn silence. They hated to have anyone call them at dinnertime. "You'd think people would know better," her mother would say. Her father had answered the phone and, almost before she realized it, they had had the same conversation they always had. "Everything's all right?" he had asked, which was always more of a statement than a question, "Oh . . . okay." Then he had told her that he was fine too, except for a little stomach trouble, and Susan had thought, In a moment I'll tell him and he won't be able to eat his dinner. But the conversation was already ending. Her father said, "Well, dear, I guess you want to speak to your mother." He always said this as soon as he could, always assumed the call was really for her mother.

And immediately her mother was on the phone, talking to her about shoes and about keeping her white dress in a plastic bag so that it wouldn't soil. "Yes, I've been doing that," Susan had lied. It had been strange to tell an everyday lie. For a moment it had seemed impossible that she wouldn't be graduating—after all, she had the dress and her mother was talking on and on about the navy-blue silk suit she was going to wear and whether or not it would rain tomorrow. Of course it wouldn't rain, Susan had thought. Her mother had already created the graduation, had insured it in advance at the department stores.

She hadn't been able to interrupt; it had seemed so pointless to say she wasn't going to get her diploma. Her mother mightn't have believed her.

At the very end her mother had asked. "Why didn't you wait to call us later? You know we're eating dinner."

"I forgot," she had said.

She saw them now. They were standing at the very edge of the lawn where they were not quite part of the celebration. She should have looked for them there in the first place, remembering the way they always hung back from crowds. Even if she had graduated, they might have chosen to stand there. How small they were! Today they looked like two faded children. Their smallness upset her, yet she was small like they were. "You'll be the tall one," they had told her when she was a little girl. She was also to have been the one who would graduate from college.

"Hello!" she cried, waving at them, coming toward them across the lawn. For a second she was sure they saw her, but then they looked away. She stopped waving. It was very difficult to walk up to them. She felt terribly exposed. Why wouldn't they look at her? Why didn't either of them move? Where was her mother's quick, dry kiss, her father's blue serge embrace? "You didn't wait in the lobby," she said lamely.

Her father cleared his throat. "We didn't feel like waiting." His voice was husky. He glanced at her mother, who was taking a Kleenex out of her pocket-book.

"I've been looking all over for you," Susan said.

There was an interminable silence. Her mother dabbed at her eyes with the Kleenex. Her father, Susan noticed now, had brought his camera. It hung around his neck on its worn leather strap. She somehow hadn't imagined he would bring it today. She hadn't imagined anything about her parents, hadn't thought of her mother putting on her new hat or her father taking the day off from the store, or their drive into the city and what they might have said to each other. She had only thought of them as they might exist for her at this moment, imagining herself confronting their abstract anger and feeling her own abstract guilt. Instead there was the camera—she remembered how her father had always told her with such pride, "This camera is as old as you are." She stared down at the grass, letting its greenness hurt her eyes.

"Well," said her father, "what have you got to say for yourself?" He was trying to sound stern. She didn't blame him. If only he could sound simply very angry, then it would be easier for her.

"I don't know what to say," she said. She couldn't look at his face.

"I see," he said bitterly.

"If you want me to say I'm sorry, then I am sorry." The words came slowly, but her voice was steady, too steady. How cold that must have sounded.

He didn't say anything. Was he going to turn her over to her mother now? She knew all too well how to act with her mother, how to pretend not to care, not to feel. But her father cried out, "What kind of trouble are you in? What kind of mess have you gotten yourself into?"

"It . . . it's not a mess exactly," Susan faltered. "It's really something sort of stupid."

Her mother glared at Susan with her reddened eyes as if she hated her. "They don't take away your diploma for nothing! You must have given them a good reason! I suppose you've been staying out all night with that boy Jerry. I know what goes on in these colleges."

Susan felt an anger that frightened her. "I flunked gym," she said. "I hope you're satisfied with that."

"Susan!" Her father clutched at her arm. "Don't talk to your mother that way!"

"If you're interested in why I flunked gym," Susan went on grimly, "it's because I didn't go to class. And I don't know why I didn't go to class. But I didn't."

"What do you mean you don't know?" said her mother. "What kind of excuse is that?"

"It's not an excuse."

"But—couldn't you have gone . . . just enough?" Her father sounded almost as if he were going to weep; his fingers tightened on her arm. She didn't answer. There was no way of answering either of them.

She let her mother's voice tear at her: "You've just thrown your education away. You had to go to a fancy college! We've always given you everything you wanted. We've given you the best. But you have no consideration, no gratitude." Her mother always spoke of consideration, gratitude—never of love; perhaps she thought they were all the same thing. "This should have been the happiest day of my life!" The voice rose hysterically.

"Marian," her father pleaded, "don't give vent."

"She let us come here today. She let us walk into this humiliation!"

"Susan," her father said, his face white, "just tell me one thing: How long have you known about this?"

"She's known about it for a month."

"I'm asking her."

Susan felt her throat tighten. "I found out yesterday. I hadn't picked up my mail for a while."

"A lie!" her mother cried triumphantly. "What do you mean you didn't pick up your mail?"

Her father spoke as if he were very tired. "You knew last night, when you called?"

Susan stared at him for a long time. "Yes," she said, "I knew." She struggled to think, to remember why she hadn't told them. If only she could find a lie. "I couldn't tell you," she said desperately.

"You let us come here instead?"

"I was going to tell you but then I couldn't. When you and mother were on the phone, I couldn't."

"I don't understand," her father said heavily. "I don't understand because I don't believe you."

Her father's words stunned her. She wanted only one thing now and that was the ability to walk away. There was nothing more to be said; she had no other reasons to give them, no energy to make her father believe her.

"You must be very proud of yourself," her father said.

She had to get away very quickly. She was trembling. If she cried, her father would believe her. But she would not cry for him.

"Excuse me," she said, "I have to return my gown." She plunged forward into the celebration.

CHAPTER FIFTEEN

THERE WAS NO one in the locker room—no one except the girl who was to check in the caps and gowns. "You're the first," she said to Susan, slipping the gown on a hanger. Then she took the cap and put it in a cardboard bin and handed Susan a white slip of paper. "There's your receipt," she said.

Susan looked at the receipt and then at the gown, no longer her gown, hanging all by itself on the rack. Her graduation was really over. Now she was supposed to go up the stairs to the lobby, walk out onto the lawn, and after that—where? If only she could stay in the locker room for a while—it was a good place to wait.

The girl was asking, "What's happening up there, anyway? I'll bet it's going to go on for hours."

It took an enormous effort to make herself answer. "Well, people are drinking punch and talking."

"Oh-h God!" the girl sighed. "I'm just dying down here. How's the punch—awful?"

"I didn't have any."

"I wish I could sneak up and get some," the girl said, yawning elaborately.

Susan found herself saying, "Why don't you? I'll stay here for a few minutes." When the girl left, she thought, she would sit at her desk. She would have a definite function, a perfectly sane reason to stay in the locker room.

The girl was looking at her suspiciously—or was she imagining that? "That's awfully nice of you. But aren't there people waiting for you or anything?"

"Oh I don't think so," she said casually. "I think they've gone." She had an image of her parents exiting by the green gate, walking heavily to their car. The girl's indecision angered her. "There's really no one waiting. Why don't you go?"

"Well . . . well, fine." The girl stood up now. "But suppose someone comes?"

"Don't worry about a thing." I'm really carrying it off, she thought.

"Just tell them I'll be back in a minute," the girl said. "This is really going to save my life," she called as she ran up the stairs.

Susan took possession of the chair and the desk. She studied the receipt the girl had given her—she was number 5214—were you supposed to keep the receipt or throw it away? She decided she wasn't the sort of person who kept receipts; if she were she probably would have graduated.

Now that the girl was gone, there was too much silence in the locker room, something ominous about all those rows of empty lockers and the gray concrete floor. Basements were always frightening. If the girl had stayed, though, she couldn't have waited here; she would have had to go upstairs before she knew where she was going. This way she had time to think, make a plan—except there was a sentence in her mind, forming and dissolving itself over and over again: "I want to die." She wondered whether that was what she really thought or whether she was just pretending to think it. She was probably pretending because the strange thing was she didn't feel any pain at all. She could think about her parents driving back to Cedarhurst and the possibility that she was never going to see them again, and feel nothing; she could even think about the possibility that she hated them, that she had been deliberately cruel—which was what they believed—and there was still no pain, no feeling, only numbness when her father had turned against her, only numbness now wondering why she was here, who she was waiting for, since obviously no one was going to come and find her. She wasn't even going to die—she would most likely end up going to the movies.

There was a clatter on the iron staircase and then the girl reappeared, crying, "Hi! Anyone come?"

"No one," Susan said. She realized guiltily that she was still sitting in the girl's chair. She stood up.

"Say," the girl asked, "is your name by any chance Susan Levitt?"

The question terrified her. "Yes . . . it is," she stammered.

"Well, there's a man in the lobby who asked if you were down here. I think it's your father."

Suddenly she felt completely calm, just as if she had never had any doubt at all that he would come for her. They might almost have arranged this meeting.

"Thanks," she said to the girl, and went to climb the stairs.

*   *   *

Her father was sitting on one of the stone benches at the end of the lobby. From a distance, he looked like one of the old men who sat every day on Riverside Drive—his body had the same weary, round-shouldered patience. She had never thought of her father as someone who was getting old. "Susie . . ." he said, standing up the moment he saw her.

She said, "Hello, Dad," and then advanced slowly toward him. It seemed such a long walk, so sedate and formal. Ten years before she would have run to him, flung her arms around his neck and cried, "I'm sorry, Daddy, I'm sorry!" She had always pleaded with her mother not to tell him that she had been bad—it wasn't his anger she had feared as a child but his sadness. "Did you do that?" he would ask with unbearable gentleness. "Yes, but I didn't *mean* to." She had really believed in her own innocence then, never doubted that once she said she was sorry she would be forgiven.

"The girl told you I was here?" he said. She nodded. "I didn't think it would take you so long to return your gown, but"—he cleared his throat—"I told your mother you probably had to wait on line."

He was frightened, she thought, and that was why he was lying a little, lying to himself—didn't he know she had to run away from them? And yet it was he and not her mother who had been able to come after her. "There wasn't a line," she said.

He was silent. She knew she had hurt him—she had done it deliberately. And then he said loudly, "I had to ask to find out which building it was. Susie!" He called out her name as if she were far away at the other end of the hall.

"Yes, Dad?" she said politely. She wondered when she had first known that her father was someone who was afraid—she had not been able to forgive him for that for a long time now. A man should not be timid; a father should not be weak. Even his gentleness was proof of his failure. Sometimes when the three of them, the family, were together, her mother would turn to her ever so slightly with a quick, sly look, a narrowing of the eyes, as if they were sharing a secret about her father. She would make her own face go blank, but would feel as guilty as if she had signaled back to her mother that she had noticed; she had always been guilty of knowing what the look had meant.

"Your mother's tired," her father said. "Maybe we'll all go out and eat now. Some nice air-conditioned place." He smiled at her sadly and waited.

"I don't feel like having any dinner," she said.

"You want to hang around here?"

"I don't know."

"Well . . ." He caught his breath heavily and tried to smile again. "I want you to come to dinner. We'll go to a nice place. We'll all feel better."

"Dad," she said helplessly, "I'm really not hungry."

"You'll be hungry later." He took a step toward her. She felt a rising panic.

"I just want to be alone!" she cried.

"You mean you don't want to be with us? I want you to come to dinner." This time he tried to make it sound like a command.

"Susan, I want you to do that for me." He took out his pocket watch and looked at it. "It's not as early as you think—it's almost six. See." He was holding up the watch.

She said, "I know what time it is."

He didn't put the watch away, but held it in the palm of his hand, staring down at it.

Somehow she had to make herself speak. "Look, Dad, I just don't think it'll be any good."

"What do you mean it won't be any good? I don't know what you mean." His voice was toneless, weary.

"But you do know!" He didn't look at her. "You know we won't just be having dinner."

"Susie," her father said, with excruciating patience, "I didn't come here to lecture you. I came to ask you to do something for me—one simple thing. I want you to come with me, now. We'll go to a restaurant with your mother, we'll sit down at a table, and we won't even talk about what happened. I told your mother we don't need to. You've done something foolish and you know you've done something foolish—you're a bright girl." She wanted to interrupt him, silence him—something—and yet she couldn't. "You must be very proud of yourself," he had said to her on the lawn, and now he was burying the thing he had said, the moment when he had perhaps hated her, with other words, and she was letting him do it—she was his daughter, as fearful as he was. She had even known all along that in the end she would go to dinner, but she wouldn't be doing it for him but because she wasn't capable of being alone or even wanting to be alone. Only her pride had made her lie before. She had been waiting for her father to come and find her from the instant she had walked away. In a little while, when it would not cost too much, she would let herself surrender.

"You know," she heard her father say, "you should have come to us in the beginning—that's where you made your mistake. Maybe we could have talked to the Dean, written a letter."

She realized then that her father still didn't believe her. "Dad—I didn't know till yesterday!"

"Well," he sighed, "whenever it was."

"It was yesterday!" she said fiercely.

He gave her a long, sad, doubtful look, and she noticed his eyes were moist. Maybe it didn't matter to him what he believed about her; maybe he would have come after her whatever he thought she had done. "We won't talk about it," he said.

"But I really didn't know until rehearsal when they called the roll, and then when I went out and got my mail—" she stopped. Her father was smiling at her painfully. "Will you please listen to me!"

Her father took out a large, very clean white handkerchief and mopped his forehead with it. His hand shook—that was because he was getting older, beginning to become an old man. She would have to remember that about him. "I'm listening," he said. "I can't make any sense out of what you say. But I'm listening."

"Do I have to make sense?"

"You did something foolish. Everyone does foolish things."

We haven't been alone for a long time, she thought; we haven't even had a conversation. This is the first conversation we've had in years.

"Talk to me, Susie. Don't make me play guessing games."

She was suddenly afraid she was going to cry. "Dad . . ."

"Am I your enemy?"

She shook her head because she couldn't speak. Her face was burning, burning, and then wet and she tasted salt on her lips, and she couldn't remember the last time she had been alone with her father because it had been too long ago.

"It's all right," she heard him say softly. "It's all right now. We've all had a terrible day, a disappointment. But we have to remember it's not the end of the world. You know, there are a few things I understand even though I am your father." And then he wiped her face with his clean white handkerchief that smelled like all the handkerchiefs of her childhood.

Her mother was waiting for them on the lawn. Her father put his arm around her shoulders and said: "Marian, I brought her back."

CHAPTER SIXTEEN

"WELL, WHERE DOES everybody want to eat?" her father said. Susan sensed a strange exhilaration in him.

"I just want something very light," said her mother. "And that's what you should have too."

He was silent for a moment. He glanced at Susan as if he were claiming her as an ally, then he rallied: "Not one of those tearoom dinners! Let's go to a *French* restaurant."

"French food?" her mother said dubiously.

Her parents had always argued about restaurants. Her mother would inevitably want something "light," her father something that would probably make him ill—he always had the sadness of a man who knew he wasn't going to win. "You'll come to me for sympathy when you're sick," her mother would say, and her father would give up so mildly, "I guess you're right," and that would be the end of it.

But tonight her father said, "We're not going to eat any boiled chicken. We're going to go to a French restaurant and get a little taste of Paris." His voice practically boomed and there was a surprised look on his face. "That's what you want to do, isn't it, Susie?" he asked her a little anxiously.

She didn't want to eat, she didn't care where they ate—but somehow she wanted her father to win this time. "That'd be fine," she said.

He put one arm around her, the other around her mother. "Come on, Marian," he said. "You'll enjoy it." Her mother was smiling ever so faintly.

For a little while, her father had become someone else, someone she remembered now: a man who was once very tall, who lifted her up in the air when he came home from the store, who protected her from the fire engines that passed in the night and from the old-clothes man—a man who had a secret life of cigars and Saturday jaunts to a place called "the track." How long had it taken him to disappear?

"What's that dish they make—*coq au vin*? That's what we'll have!" he cried. "Susie, you must know a good French restaurant."

She could only think of one. "*La Lune d'Argent*," she said, and wondered why the name made her a little uneasy. Then she remembered—Jerry. "Maybe we'd better not . . ." But she hadn't thought about Jerry for days—she couldn't quite remember his face now when she tried to. It would be strange to go to his restaurant. She saw herself sitting with her parents in that subdued, elegant room—three small people. They would make her feel more hopelessly an outsider than Jerry had.

"Something wrong with it, Susie?"

"Oh . . . it's just that maybe it's a little expensive."

Her father laughed. "If you say it's a good restaurant, that's where we'll eat."

"Maybe it's a very dressy place," her mother said.

"Don't worry about that, Marian. You look fine."

They were both smiling at her, they were waiting for her to say that it was a good restaurant. "It's a very good restaurant," she said.

So they went to *La Lune d'Argent* and were ushered to one of the ridiculous little tables—"For midgets," her father commented, loudly enough for the waiter to hear, and her mother stared, fascinated, at all the bare backs and bare shoulders of the ladies— "They wear a lot of black in the city, don't they?" Her father, who was on what Kay would have called a "French kick," seized the menu and studied it for a long time. "What's this dish?" he would ask Susan, and she would translate. "Well, then," he would say with pride, "shall we have some—*haricots verts*?"

"Susan certainly seems to know French," said her mother.

Susan very nearly answered, "Not bad for an English major," but that would have reminded them of the graduation. They all had to pretend now that they had forgotten it, or that it had never happened. It was just as her father had said: "We won't talk about it." But there was still that redness in her mother's eyes and probably in her own, and she didn't know how she was going to eat this dinner—her father wanted to order her duck *à l'orange* because he remembered she liked duck; "But have anything you want," he added shyly.

"Such fancy dishes," her mother said. "After a few months in Paris you'll appreciate some good home cooking."

They both kept talking to her about Paris; they seemed to have decided that that was a safe topic. Of course, they didn't really want her to go, but they were somehow able to reassure themselves by imagining a humdrum existence for her even there. Her mother pictured her with stomach aches and a terrible laundry problem; her father advised her to "make the most of it," not to spend too much time reading in her hotel room. Her stay in Paris was so much more real to them than it was to her.

She listened to them, smiling, nodding occasionally, trying to oblige them, to be the daughter they should have had, docile, innocent, respectful—the Paris lies had already begun, she thought. Truth was an impossibility. They were her mother and father, and they would never, never know who she was, how she lived. Her silence must have disturbed them—every now and then she caught a frightened look in their eyes, as if they were asking, Will she do that? Is that what it will be like?

Her father was signaling to the waiter now. "Gar-song! Gar-song!" he called.

The waiter glided to their table. "M'sieu?" he said discreetly.

"Listen," her father said, "I think we'll have a little something to drink before dinner."

"Cocktails, M'sieu?"

"Well, I'd like something sort of special. You see," he said loudly, "it's a special festive occasion." He gave Susan and her mother a rather defiant look. "My daughter just graduated from college."

She wanted to run from the table, she wanted to weep. Why was her father doing this to her? Why was he humiliating her now? Was it because he knew he had won? He would make her hate him for winning. He would make her hate him.

"Perhaps some champagne?" the waiter suggested.

"Champagne—yes, that's what we'll have." For the first time her father sounded a little nervous. The waiter glided away. "A little champagne won't hurt us." Her mother's face had gone blank.

They sat in silence until the waiter returned bearing the bottle of champagne wedged into a bucket of ice, the three glasses. Then there was the ritual of pulling the cork—it popped just as if this were a real celebration; the champagne foamed into her glass before she could tell her father she didn't want it.

Her father lifted his glass. "To Susan's happiness," he said huskily. After a moment, her mother lifted hers too, and didn't smile; there was a pleading softness in her face.

They were doing this because this was what they thought she wanted. They were celebrating her graduation. They were doing this because they loved her.

CHAPTER SEVENTEEN

SHE WAS STILL wearing her white dress. Her image confronted her, submerged in the blue chrome façade of the Riverside Café—a bluish girl in white. She was going to look quite misplaced sitting in the Riverside. A week ago she might have gone back to her room to change. But now it didn't matter what she wore. This was her last night, already slipping away from her.

At dinner, her father had said, "Come back to Cedarhurst with us, Susie. It'll be easier than taking the train tomorrow with a suitcase." He had suggested it very casually, but she had known how much they both wanted her home that night. It would have been easier in so many ways to have gone with them, except that then everything would have been so incomplete. "But I have an appointment," she had said, and she hadn't felt that she was lying. If you knew where people would be at a certain time and you knew that you had to see them, it was almost the same as having an appointment.

The Riverside Café was practically empty. A solitary boy was playing the bowling machine and the few anonymous drinkers at the bar were watching an ancient movie on television. As

Susan walked in, three characters on the screen burst into a song: *"Lookie, lookie, lookie / Here comes Cookie . . ."*

"Susan . . ." Her name was spoken very quietly by someone who had come up close behind her—a voice she knew. She stood quite still for a moment, feeling an odd little shiver run through her, and then turned.

"Peter!"

He was standing poised like a juggler, a glass of beer balanced in each hand. *"Lookie, lookie, lookie / Here comes Cookie,"* he sang half under his breath, studying her with amused gray eyes, her face briefly, then her dress, then her face again. "Should I congratulate you," he said, "or not?"

"Maybe you'd better not," she said, turning her face away.

"Kay told me what happened. Anyway, I like you in that dress."

"I'll never wear it again," she said gravely.

He was laughing. "Because I like it?"

"No. Other reasons." Peter took a gulp of beer from one of the glasses. "Is Kay here?" she said, wishing she had asked it sooner.

"In the back booth," he said. "I didn't think she was expecting you."

"Tonight's my last night. I haven't said good-bye to her."

"She's a bit under the weather. In fact, I was going to take her home and then go to a party. Maybe you'd like to go."

"I don't know." She had to stop herself from saying yes. "I'll see what Kay wants to do."

"It would be better than killing the rest of the night here."

She followed Peter now as he loped toward the back of the Riverside, his walk more ungainly than usual. He's a little drunk, she thought, feeling a disturbing tenderness for him, for his stooping shoulders, his massive head. Last week she had watched him walk down Broadway and hadn't recognized him at first. Even now she hardly knew him, yet he was someone she would remember; she had come here to say good-bye to him, too. She wondered if he would go off to the party if she couldn't go with him.

Suddenly Peter stopped and faced her. "You didn't come over this week."

"I was busy." This was her last night, she reminded herself, a night when nothing could happen. "Did you think I would?" she asked boldly.

"I thought about it now and then." He wasn't smiling.

She felt ridiculously, dangerously happy. He had wanted to see her—she would remember that. They walked the rest of the way to Kay's booth in silence, not even glancing at each other.

Kay had burrowed herself into the darkest corner of the booth. "Kay!" Peter called sternly, "I've brought a friend of yours." He set a glass of beer down in front of her.

Kay raised her head and moved slightly out of the darkness. She stared at Susan as if she weren't quite sure she knew her. "I told you I'd get drunk," she said.

"Well, I guess you did."

Kay looked so much like a child—not a drunken child but a sleepy one; her cheeks were flushed, her eyes innocent and vulnerable without glasses. "Do you mind?" she said in an elaborate British accent, drawing out the vowels. Susan shook her head. Kay giggled. "Do sit down, duckie."

"Who are you playing now?" Peter inquired pleasantly. "Eliza Doolittle?"

"No. That's a part for someone very beautiful."

Susan sat down next to Kay. Shyly, she touched Kay's shoulder. "Hey there, duckie," she whispered.

Kay's head dropped. "I'm the old charwoman."

Peter was frowning. "You ought to go home, you know, Kay."

"I don't want to."

"I'll walk you home and put you to bed."

"I will *not* be put!" Kay's voice shook. "I will not be put anywhere."

Peter shrugged. "Have it your own way."

"That's right, I will. Besides," Kay said, "Susan's here. Lovely Susan in her white dress. Peter, let's take Susan to the party."

"I thought you didn't want to go," he said.

"I do want to go. I'm drunk enough now. I won't embarrass you by being morbid."

Peter's face was expressionless. "Drink your beer," he said.

Obediently Kay picked up her glass. "Susan needs something to drink too, Peter."

"Oh, that's all right," Susan said hastily.

But Peter asked, "What would you like to drink, Susan?" as if that were a very important question.

"Beer . . . I suppose," she said reluctantly and reached for her purse. She didn't want him to buy her a drink.

Peter's hand closed around her wrist. "This is on me," he said. "What would you really like to have?"

"Just beer." Why didn't he take his hand away? Was Kay watching?

"Don't worry," Kay said, "Peter got his check today. He's bought me hundreds of drinks. When someone wants to buy you a drink, Susan, you must never, never refuse."

"I'll get Susan a Pernod," Peter said.

"De-finitely."

"What's a Pernod?" Susan asked helplessly.

"It tastes like licorice," Kay giggled.

Peter was smiling. "Your first Pernod!"

"Your first Pernod!" Kay sang. "You'll get very drunk just like me."

Peter stood up. He had pulled his wallet out of his pocket. Now he took four dollars from it and put the money down on the table in front of Susan. "I owe you this," he said. Before she could speak, he walked away. The money lay untouched in front of her. It seemed unthinkable to pick it up, put it in her purse.

"Well, did you make the graduation scene? Did your parents have you for dinner?" There was a harshness in Kay's voice. It was strange that drinking didn't mellow Kay—it seemed to make her more bitter, less afraid to hate.

"It wasn't so bad," Susan said quietly. She didn't feel like talking about any of it—especially about her parents. Her father with his glass of champagne—if she talked about that, it might sound almost funny and she'd feel dirty if anyone laughed.

"You're keeping all your secrets," Kay said, "and that's because I'm being disgusting—oh yes, I know I am. And you're coming on like such a young lady. . . . I don't even know why you're here or how you got here. I've been watching the street all day and no one came in."

"I wanted to see you, so I came," Susan said, hating the bright voice she used. Was that how sober people talked to drunken ones? Perhaps she should get drunk herself. She wondered how many drinks it would take. "Kay, I'm going back to Cedarhurst tomorrow. And then there'll be the ship—but everything will be formal and ridiculous."

"I wasn't planning to come to the ship." Susan felt a stab of pain. Kay was smiling. "But I'll send you a telegram if you like. Would you like a funny telegram?"

"Sure," Susan said unsteadily.

"I'll have to start thinking of one . . ." Kay's voice trailed off; she shut her eyes and then abruptly pitched forward, burying her head in her arms. "Dizzy . . ." she murmured.

"Kay . . ." Susan shook her gently, but there was no response. "Kay, do you want to sleep?" This time she heard her moan a little. What was the point of waking Kay up, extracting a last night from her—what right had she to do that? Susan leaned back against the booth's green plastic upholstery, the weariness that had been with her for hours washing over her now. Everything had a perfect, terrifying clarity: the cars rushing by on Broadway, Kay's head lying like an object on the table, Peter miles away at the bar—the beautifully preserved world almost lifelike under its layer of ice. . . .

Eleven o'clock now. Her night was vanishing. She was sitting in the Riverside Café, watching the same door she had watched so many other nights, the door Kay had watched, sitting and waiting for something to happen to her, someone to come in.

Susan found herself standing up. She walked down the long

aisle between the booths, past the bowling machine, the cigarette machine, the jukebox. Peter was standing alone at the bar—he didn't see her coming. She knew there would be a stiffness between them at first; she also knew that it would pass.

When she called his name, he turned around so quickly that she wasn't ready for him. "I thought I'd like to sit at the bar." The words she said sounded wrong, of course—anything would have sounded wrong.

"I was just going to bring you your drink," she heard him say.

"Oh . . . that's all right."

"Well, have a seat if you want to sit here." Peter motioned at the bar stool next to him. "Bring me another beer, Al," he called to the bartender. Susan perched herself on the bar stool. "Didn't you and Kay want to talk?" Peter said.

Kay fell asleep."

"Not very interesting for you. Do you want to put up with me instead, or would you just like to sit at the bar?"

"Oh, I'll talk to you," she said brightly.

Suddenly Peter smiled. "Don't you want your drink?" He shoved a glass of ice water at her, then a shot glass with something yellow in it. "You see, I did order it. I would have gotten it to you sooner or later."

"Is this the Pernod?" Susan picked up the shot glass—somehow she couldn't quite bring herself to touch the glass of ice water.

"Wait! Don't drink it like that. You have to mix it." Peter took the shot glass away from her and poured the yellow liquid into the ice water. The water clouded, became less alarming. She raised the glass to her lips.

"It's good," she said dubiously. Peter was staring at her, not smiling any longer. "This is a nice drink. You know, I don't like the way most liquor tastes. Maybe I'll get drunk tonight."

Peter leaned toward her. "Do you want to?"

"I don't know. I thought I might before." How gray his eyes were, a very cold gray.

"Why would you get drunk?"

"Oh . . . to find out what it's like. To—make contact, really." There was a frightening intensity about the way Peter was listening, drawing words from her as if he were pulling thread from a spool. "Is Pernod a very strong drink?" He didn't answer. She picked up her glass again; balancing it on the palm of one hand, she turned it around and around. "Such a cloudy yellow . . ."

"You look like my wife, my ex-wife." She sat motionless. "The way you hold that glass . . . and that dress. . . . Did you know I was married once?"

"Well . . . yes—I did know." She didn't know what to do, whether to put the glass down or not.

"I suppose it's common knowledge." Susan said nothing. "Funny that I ordered you Pernod—that's what Carol would always have."

"Is that her name?"

"Yes. Carol. You don't know whether you like looking like my ex-wife," he said.

"It's just strange." It was like looking like someone who had died, she thought, and yet it was somehow exciting to know that you had a particular look; it was proof that you existed, had a face, a shape.

"Her hair was a little longer than yours." She felt as if he had touched her, as if he had put his hand on her hair. And nothing had happened, nothing at all. Peter sat just as he had been sitting, holding his beer—not even his eyes moved.

"Were you married for a long time?" she asked shyly.

"Two years. I couldn't stand being married. Couldn't fall asleep at night. I'd get up, go out. . . . It wasn't her fault."

"Where would you go?"

"Bars," he said. "A lot of places I can't remember. Sometimes I'd walk for hours—I didn't have a car then. What difference does it make where I went?" he cried. "What a question!"

She could imagine Peter prowling through the city, could see him standing on a street at five o'clock in the morning utterly alone—maybe even happy at that moment in a strange sort of way. What would it be like to love someone like that? Probably awful. Suppose you wanted to go wandering with him and you knew that he would never take you along and night after night you watched him go—and you were never able to say, "Take me with you." What was it like for Kay? she wondered. She really couldn't even imagine Kay and Peter alone, couldn't think of them as lovers—and yet they made love and Kay loved Peter and Peter loved . . . no one, except maybe his ex-wife, or the memory, the image of her. If you couldn't love people, you turned them into images.

"Stop thinking," Peter demanded. "It's very unfriendly. I don't like to sit and watch myself being dissected." He took the glass out of her hand. "You don't mind if I finish your drink, do you?"

"No." It gave her an odd pleasure to watch him drink from her glass.

When it was empty he put it down on the bar. "You shouldn't let people take things away from you," he said. "You shouldn't allow people like me to depress you."

"You haven't depressed me."

"I think I wanted to. When you walked over to me, I should have said, 'Susan, you shouldn't even be in this place tonight. Let me take you away from here, let's celebrate . . .'"

"Oh stop!" she said, laughing.

"But isn't that what you expected?"

"No!"

"You're lying. Women always expect that from a man."

"I didn't expect anything," she said.

He was silent. "You know," he said solemnly, "I think I'm angry with you because you're going way. . . . We might have had a chance to make each other miserable for a while—I suppose that's the way it would have worked out."

"I don't know," she said faintly.

"I do know."

Someone plunged past them. The Riverside Café turned itself on again—suddenly the jukebox was pounding and a man was shouting, "Beer! Beer!"; the balls in the bowling machine were crashing into the pins; the bartender was wiping glasses. With a feeling of panic, she noticed that the door to Broadway was swinging back and forth a little as if someone had just left. She made herself look back at Kay's booth and saw that it was empty. "Peter! Kay's gone!" she cried. She slid down from the stool and rushed out of the bar into the street.

CHAPTER EIGHTEEN

K<small>AY WAS HALFWAY</small> up the block. She didn't stop when Susan called to her, but kept on walking, slowly, aimlessly, like someone blindfolded. "Kay! Wait!" She knew how it had been for Kay—how Kay had awakened from her sleep and found herself alone and walked to the bar to be with them, and how, when she had seen them, there must have been something about the way they looked together—the way their heads were turned perhaps, the angle at which they leaned toward each other—that made it seem as if they were shutting her out, that she was isolate, that no one would hear her if she spoke, notice if she passed. "Please wait, Kay!" Susan ran now in her new white high-heeled shoes. Somewhere behind her, Peter's voice cried, "Susan!" and she realized that he must have followed her out of the bar, but she kept going. In a moment she was going to overtake Kay; she would ask her what's wrong, what's the matter, what do you mean leaving us like that? "Kay, wait!" Kay had halted on the corner, trapped there because the cars kept coming, the light hadn't changed. Susan stopped running and walked the rest of the way—no one was supposed to run after anyone else.

"Hey, Kay . . . where are you going?" Standing next to each other now, they might have been two people who had been wandering Broadway together.

But Kay wouldn't stop watching the cars. "Across the street," she said.

"Going to the Southwick Arms?"

Kay shrugged.

"Going to Bickford's for coffee, Kay? Why don't you come back to the Riverside?" Her voice lost some of its lightness.

"No!" Kay said hoarsely.

"Would you like me to go somewhere else with you?"

"I just want to cross the street."

"Listen, Kay . . ." Listen to what? she thought. She was stalling for time, a moment; the light was changing. Why was she so afraid of not being able to sound indifferent?

"Well, ladies, what's happening?" Suddenly Peter was present. She heard Kay make a stifled, wordless sound and saw that all the cars had stopped. Kay stepped off the curb, hesitated, then began to cross Broadway. "What the hell is going on?" Peter shouted, running out after her. He grasped Kay's arm and yanked her back to the curb. "Would you mind telling me the meaning of this performance!"

Kay looked at Peter, then at Susan; tears were wetting her face. "Good night," she whispered.

"It's very difficult to hear you," Peter said. "Could you possibly speak a little louder?" But Kay shut her eyes and stood before them mute, a prisoner waiting to be sentenced. "Christ! why is it always this way with you? Why all this silence? You make me feel like a tyrant!"

"You're . . . not," Kay gasped.

"Now stop playing the orphan girl. People can't bear victims, Kay. Goddammit, you're always—effacing yourself!"

Susan had never seen Peter so angry—but maybe anger could reach Kay. She heard Kay dully recite: "I know what I am."

"You don't know anything. You're an idiot."

"I'm drunk. I can't—"

"Yes, tonight you're a drunken idiot. Look at you!" He seized her by the shoulder and held her at arms' length. "Crazy Jane! Someone ought to wash your face for you."

Kay laughed brokenly. "But not you."

"I didn't say that—I said *someone*." Peter drew Kay closer to him; he brushed her hair back from her forehead. "Come on. The three of us will go back to the bar and have another drink."

"No—you go back with Susan. I can't make it in there."

"No one can," Peter said. "It's a terrible place."

Susan stepped forward. "We'll go anywhere you like, Kay. But you've got to come with us."

Kay hadn't taken her eyes off Peter. "Go with Susan," she said to him.

"Kay!" Susan cried out.

Kay turned to her. "Just don't tell him about the drawings—that's all."

"Kay," Susan said desperately, "I *love* you."

"Not necessary," Kay muttered. "Not necessary." She shook her head.

"I wanted you to know that."

Kay's eyes avoided hers. When she finally spoke, she said, "Can I cross the street now? I want to go home."

They walked Kay to the hotel, took her to her room in the South-wick Arms Hotel. Was that what Kay meant by home—a room? She had told them she didn't want them to come with her, but they had made her walk between them for four blocks—she stumbled a bit, said nothing at all. Would it have been kinder to have let her go alone? They rode up with Kay in the elevator to the sixth floor; they escorted her down the corridor. A lot of the doors were half-open because it was a warm night—you could look in and see people alive in their little garishly lit boxes. A party was going on in one of the rooms. "A gala night," Peter remarked. Then they waited in the corridor while Kay groped for something in her purse. "I can't find the key," she kept saying. "I don't have it. I can't find the key." "Having trouble, Kay?" Peter asked. No answer. Across the hall someone was being very angry in Spanish.

At last Kay found the key and opened her door. But then she just stood there, outside her room.

"All right, Kay?" Peter said wearily. He wanted it to be over now, Susan thought—they had brought Kay to her room, why wouldn't she go in? The next thing he was probably going to say was "So long. See you tomorrow." And the door would close. And that would be all. Good-bye to Kay—she hadn't even said that yet.

Kay hadn't moved. She gave them a dazed look. "I forgot to leave my light on."

"Kay," Susan said gently, "I'll turn it on. I know where it is." She stepped past Kay into the darkness and felt along the wall for the switch. "I've got it, Kay!" she called.

The room was suddenly much too bright—she could see its sadness too well. This was a room she never could have lived in. This was the last time she would stand here, her last view of the rented, indestructible furniture, the debris of Kay's life, the pictures Kay had tacked on the green wallpaper that she would not have chosen herself—no answer for her in the little nun's starved face.

Peter was still standing in the doorway, but Kay had come all the way into the room. She wandered around at first like a child in a strange house, touching the back of a chair, fingering a book; then she stopped and stared at Susan.

"All right now, Kay?" Peter demanded.

Kay's face was flushed, exhausted; her eyes kept closing. "Susan . . ." she said slowly, her voice low and sweet, "I don't have any coffee for you. I used it all up."

"Oh Kay—it doesn't matter." She could hardly get the words out.

"I should have saved some," Kay said vaguely. Then she seemed to be staring at the wallpaper. "You know," she said, "my walls are green just like the Riverside's. The same green"—her voice rose—"the same green walls. All the walls in my life are the same color!"

"Kay!" Peter said from the doorway. "You ought to get some rest now. You ought to go to sleep."

"I know," Kay murmured.

"Why don't you go and lie down?" He walked into the room and took Kay by the arm. "Come on—get into bed," he said sternly. Kay giggled. "Come on."

"I'm really your daughter, Peter," Kay said, letting him lead her across the room. "I'm really your daughter." She kicked off her shoes and laid herself down on top of the rumpled blanket of her unmade bed.

"Aren't you going to take some of your clothes off?" said Peter. "You don't look very comfortable."

Kay had closed her eyes. "I'm comfortable."

Susan noticed Kay's bedspread lying on the floor at the foot of the bed. She went and picked it up, then draped it over Kay, tucking it in around her.

"What are you doing that for?" Kay whispered.

"Oh, I don't know. It seemed like a good idea."

Kay smiled slightly. "You must both kiss me good night—will you?"

"Of course." Her voice shook. She bent down and kissed Kay quickly on the forehead.

"And Peter—leave the light on." Kay opened her eyes and reached for his hand.

"Any other instructions?" Peter laughed.

Kay was silent for a moment. "Yes," she said gravely. "I think you should get the car and take Susan for a ride." Her hand slipped away from Peter's. "I'm awfully drunk," she said, just before she fell asleep.

They stood in front of the Southwick Arms Hotel. It was one o'clock in the morning now and there was a wind from the river blowing up 113th Street. Peter was trying to light a cigarette, but the wind kept putting the matches out. "The hell with it!" he said, tossing the cigarette away. Then he looked at her. She wasn't afraid of his eyes. It was the wind that made her shiver a little. "Are you cold?" he asked.

"No. Not really. I feel—very awake," she said.

"So do I." He was smiling. Suddenly his face looked very young. "Susan, would you like to go somewhere?"

"Yes," she said quietly, "I think I would."

CHAPTER NINETEEN

THE NIGHT HAD transfigured the road—the highway her parents had traveled a few hours ago—now, for her, a road without end, without even landmarks. She was sitting in the front seat of the car next to Peter, watching the car's lights whiten the darkness ahead of them, always the same whiteness to drive into and everything dark beyond it, the shapes of trees, houses, to be felt rather than seen. He said that maybe they would find a beach very early in the morning, they would get out and watch the sun come up. But even if they didn't, it wouldn't matter. She was traveling fast, she was riding through the center of night—she was with Peter, next to him, and yet alone. The car was making the same machine-gun sound she had heard four days ago. Sometimes it would stall, sometimes it rushed forward violently—but she had no sense of danger. Peter began to drive even faster. She leaned back against the seat and shut her eyes. She could feel the speed now as if it were a force inside her.

The car wasn't moving. Susan woke with a start. There was light everywhere, harsh gray light, and a no-colored sky. "Peter?" She put out her hand, but he wasn't there. She sat up, her heart beating wildly, and looked out the window. Little orange and green flags were flapping in the wind and a sign said Esso. She was in a gas station. The hood of the car was up, and she saw Peter standing near a gas pump talking to a man. She groped for her shoes—she couldn't remember taking them off—opened the door and climbed out of the car. "Peter!" she called. He turned and waved his hand at her and she walked unsteadily toward him, on legs that were not quite hers yet. It was terribly cold. The wind kept whipping at her dress. Peter's face looked gray, older, maybe because of the light or because he needed a shave. "What's happening, Peter?" she said.

Peter shrugged wearily. "The car seems to have had it."

"What's wrong with it?"

"Like I said," the gas station man put in, "you can have it fixed."

"Yeah, I know," Peter said. "Seventy-five dollars." He looked at Susan. "Let's go and have some coffee. There's a diner across the road. I'm going to leave the car here for a few minutes," he said to the gas station man. "Is that all right?"

"It's all right with me," said the man, "just as long as you can drive it out."

"I'll drive it out," Peter said stiffly. "Come on, Susan."

She followed him across an expanse of concrete that was gray too, she noticed. Even her dress looked gray.

"Did the car break down?" she asked with an effort. The problem of the car didn't seem real somehow.

"It's still running, but it's pretty far gone," Peter said grimly.

"Oh. But what's wrong?"

"Transmission," he said.

"Is that serious?"

"Yes." Peter sounded as if he didn't want her to ask any more questions. He was walking very quickly, walking across the road, away from her, as if she had turned into an enemy. She was completely awake now. She folded her arms and held them tightly against her body for warmth; she didn't try to catch up with him.

When Peter reached the diner, he waited for her, holding the door open, but his face was bleak, remote. Susan thought the waitress gave them an odd look when Peter ordered the two coffees. She was suddenly very conscious that she hadn't combed her hair, that her dress was badly creased, that it was five-thirty in the morning and she was sitting in a diner in an unknown town miles away from her room, her suitcases, her life.

For a long time Peter stared out of the window and stirred his coffee. "I'm going to sell the car," he said at last.

There was such a deadness in his voice that she could think of nothing to say. All she could do was ask: "Can't you have it fixed, Peter?" which was no better than saying nothing. He didn't answer. "The man said it could be fixed."

"Yes," Peter said bitterly. "For seventy-five dollars."

"Can't you get it?"

"No, I can't," he said. "Susan, I'm twenty-nine years old and eight hundred dollars in debt—that's a nice adult sum, isn't it? And the car's a—toy, you know . . . just a distraction. It wouldn't even pay to fix it. It cost me a hundred; now it's worth about forty.

And it's old. Every few months something else is going to fall apart. . . . Why are you looking so depressed?" he demanded. "You should be encouraging me."

"I can't imagine you without the car," she said.

"Oh you see it as a tragedy—like the Lone Ranger shooting his horse. What was the name of that horse? Come on—you know it." He looked hard at her and tried to laugh.

But she wouldn't say it. She was thinking about how it would be for Peter now, how he would wake up in his apartment at noon each day and find that more dust had settled overnight, how he would go out for breakfast because there weren't any clean cups, how he would drift up and down Broadway until he was tired enough to sleep again.

"Think!" Peter said sternly.

"It was Silver," she said. "*Hi-yo Silver! The Lone Ranger rides again . . .*" The words caught in her throat.

A smile flickered across Peter's face. "Very good."

"Useful information," she said. But he was looking out of the window again. She drank about half of her cup of coffee.

"You know," she heard him say, "if I thought the car would last—even a few more days—I'd be tempted to get into it now and just keep going."

"I wonder where we'd end up," she said.

Peter turned, his eyes cold. "Oh—did I invite you?"

Her mouth quivered; she didn't trust her voice, her face. She picked up the cup she had just put down.

"I thought you had to get back to your suitcases."

"That's right."

"Well, the real problem anyway is whether or not the car can make it back to New York—that is the real problem," he said loudly. "Susan?"

"Yes."

"You can either take your chances with me or catch a train. I can give you a little money toward the fare."

She was silent. She ought to tell him she'd take the train; that was what she ought to tell him. "I'll take my chances," she said unsteadily.

Peter laughed. "You want the honor of being my last passenger—is that it?" He laid his hand heavily on her shoulder. "Is that it, Susan?"

She wouldn't look at him. "I don't want anything," she said.

"I think I'll sell the car today," Peter said, as if he hadn't heard her, "get it over with. There are a lot of places in the Bronx that buy used cars—near Yankee Stadium. A hideous section. You wouldn't want to go to the Bronx." His hand rested on her shoulder a moment longer; then he looked at his watch. "We ought to go now," he said. "I'll have to drive slowly."

We're not going to fly this time, she thought.

"Better finish your coffee," Peter said.

Her anger had left her. There was something she wanted to say. She needed only a little more courage, a little more silence. But her cup was empty; now Peter stood up and began to search his pockets for change. "I'm finished," she said sadly. Then she stood up, too.

Peter put two dimes down on the counter. "Let's go," he said.

"Peter . . . " If she didn't say it now, she wouldn't say it—it could not be said without risk. "Peter, if you're going to sell the car this morning—well, why don't I go with you?"

He didn't make it easy for her, didn't answer right away. "You have a desire to go to the Bronx."

"That's right," she said.

"Just for the ride." His eyes met hers—she didn't turn from them. "I'll think about it," he said at last.

When they left the diner they discovered that it had begun to rain—a fine rain that drifted down on them like mist. It wasn't windy any more. Instead there was a great stillness. Not a car moved upon the highway. The trees shook softly, and across the road the little flags hung sodden on their lines like garish laundry. They were walking to the car very slowly as if they had all the time in the world.

"Do you mind getting wet?" Peter said.

"No." Susan smiled. She wanted to be wet, drenched, to walk under the enormous sky—a different sky than the one you saw in the city in little bits and pieces. For once there was no urgency to rush to a dry place.

CHAPTER TWENTY

THEY WERE IN a part of the city she had never seen before. "The rear end of New York," Peter called it. They had driven through Harlem, crossed an ugly bridge that squatted over an ugly, sluggish river, and now there were signs that said they were near Yankee Stadium. It had stopped raining hours ago, but there was a grayness here that was dense, smoky.

She had a feeling that everything was going to go wrong, that somewhere in one of these desolate streets a bitter point was going to be made—and the car had to be sold, left here; they could not turn it back and drive away. Its machine-gun sound was louder than ever, louder than the radio Peter had just turned on, louder than Peter's voice that had suddenly begun to talk away at her about how they were going to find the right place, get the best deal. He didn't have to sell it to a junk dealer. He didn't have to settle for forty dollars. The car was worth more, he kept saying, more. She wanted to shut the radio off, press her hand against his mouth. On the road, before, he hadn't been afraid of silence.

Because they were looking for the right place, they didn't stop anywhere. They drove slowly down every block—Used Cars!

Used Cars!, cars that were dead, *Useless* Cars!, useless toy hulks piled one on top of another waiting to be burned, reduced to metal. Then they found themselves passing the bridge again. "Well, looks like we're going around in circles," Peter said. "Not much point in that, is there? Is there?"

"I guess not," she said softly.

They stopped for a red light and Peter looked at his watch. "It's getting late—almost ten. What time do you have to get your things out of the dorms?"

"Oh, twelve," she said, "one—don't worry about it."

"You have to get back," he said. The light changed. Peter jammed his foot down on the gas pedal and the car jolted forward. "Sorry," he muttered, but he didn't slow down. He stopped the car at the first car lot they came to. "We'll try this one," he said. "They're all crooks anyway. You wait here—all right?" He touched her arm.

"All right," she said.

"Better if I go in alone." He got out of the car and slammed the door; the sound the door made, the clash of metal upon metal, kept ringing in her ears. Now he walked in front of the window, now he crossed the pavement, now he was going across the lot, a man walking all by himself between the rows of cars; now she sat in the front seat of the intricate, doomed machine that belonged to him and waited; she was somewhere in the Bronx and it was morning and the radio was playing its particular music—and the only strangeness about it was that none of it seemed strange at all.

*   *   *

They didn't want the car, he told her—"The bastards! Stupid bastards!" There was a flatness about his anger. He sat in the front seat staring straight ahead.

"Tell me what happened." Oh, Peter, look at me, she thought, look at me. . . . "Wouldn't they give you enough money?"

"I told you," he said, "they didn't want it. They didn't offer me anything. Not a cent. Nothing. Don't you understand?"

She was silent. Then she said, "That was only the first place."

"The car has no value," Peter said quietly. Suddenly he reached forward and turned the volume dial of the radio all the way up. "The next bastards will hear us coming!" And then the car was moving again.

On the next block there was another place. "We'll see what *their* story is," Peter said grimly. But after they pulled up, he just sat at the wheel for a while smoking a cigarette. A dog was barking wildly and there was the stench of burnt rubber in the air. She saw a man sitting in front of a trailer in an enormous decrepit armchair. Above the man's head, there was a large sign: MATTY'S SQUARE DEAL AUTO LOT. USED CARS! AUTOMOBILE PARTS! At the bottom of the sign, in smaller letters were the words: *Beware of the dog!*

"Peter," she said, "don't try this one. Let's go somewhere else."

"But we're here." He stabbed his cigarette again and again into the ash tray.

"It's not a good place!" she cried. "I know it's not!"

For the moment that his eyes met hers, she saw the pain in them. Then he put his hand on the door. "It won't take long," he said.

The dog was barking and barking. The man waited in his enormous chair.

When Peter came back to the car, he shut off the radio. "It gets better," he said. "It gets better and better."

This time she asked no questions.

After a while, he turned to her. "Susan," he said, "open the glove compartment, will you? I've got a hammer in there."

"A hammer?" she said.

"Go on—open it."

"Are you going to fix something, Peter?"

He took the hammer from her. "No. There's something else I want to do." He got out of the car and walked behind it.

"Peter . . ."

He struck the rear window with the hammer, shattering the glass, struck it again after a moment, then again, then one of the side windows, then he walked around to the window on the other side. . . . It was all done without violence, as if he were performing a ceremony. Then he dropped the hammer on the pavement and got back into the car. "It's still mine," he said to her.

Unable to speak, she nodded.

He said, "I'm sorry if I frightened you."

"I wasn't frightened." She hadn't been frightened at all—only sad, sad . . . but he wouldn't want to know about her sadness—she had come with him "just for the ride."

Peter turned the key in the ignition. "Well, I guess we'll find a junk yard." The machine gun began to fire again. He was backing the car into the street. "That man over there," he said, "actually had a sense of humor. He said if he had a car like this he wanted to get rid of, he'd just drive it over a cliff."

The old man who had come out to look at the car said, finally, "To tell you the truth, mister, I can't give you much for it. I can give you five dollars."

"Five dollars . . ." His eyes half-closed, Peter slowly shook his head. "Five dollars . . ."

That was worse, she thought, than nothing at all. Much worse. A flat five dollars. If only he wouldn't settle for that—but he was going to. She knew he was going to. But the car could still run. It was big, black, powerful. It hadn't died yet. It could still carry them away from here back over the bridge. And its radio played so well. Peter could drive the car to the other side of the bridge and then abandon it.

"Ain't much demand for these here parts—an old car like this."

"They don't make cars like this any more," Peter said—the last time he would say that to anyone, she thought.

"That's why there ain't no demand for parts. Got to settle for scrap value. See all the scrap I got here right now, young lady?" Now the old man addressed himself to her, gesturing with a stiff arm. "Can't even get a good price for it these days."

Peter was taking a long look at the yard, the half acre of dismembered, rusting machinery.

"Listen, mister, I ain't trying to cheat you!" the old man called out to him.

Peter was staring at the car now. "No," he said slowly. "As a matter of fact, you've made the best offer yet. Don't you think so, Susan?" But she knew he didn't expect an answer; he hadn't taken his eyes off the car. "All right," he said. "Sold for five dollars."

The old man said fine, he'd be right back with the money and the papers—there were papers to fill out. Everything had to be legal. Peter said, "Just don't forget the cash," and the old man went off laughing. Then they stood and waited, and Peter told her that if she'd left anything in the car she'd better get it, and she said she had everything.

The old man came back with the papers and Peter started to fill them out and sign them. "If you ain't legal, you're heading for trouble—right?" said the old man, and winked at her. "Hey, mister," he said. "What about all this stuff you got back here in the car. You going to take it?"

"No," Peter said curtly.

"You got a lot of stuff."

"I won't be needing it. You can take your papers," he said.

"Here's your five," said the old man.

Peter didn't put the bill in his pocket; he kept crumpling it up in his hand. The old man was already busy taking the license plate off the car with his screwdriver. "Let's go," Peter said to her at last. "Let's go." He started walking fast; she followed him.

"Wait, mister!" the old man shouted.

"We're in a hurry."

"I gotta give you your license plate."

"Forget it!" Peter walked a little faster.

"Hey, *mister*!" The old man caught up with them. "You gotta take your license plate, mister."

Peter stopped and faced him. "Why don't you just melt it down!" he cried. "It'll melt!"

The old man stared at him in bewilderment. "It's the law, mister." Angrily he thrust the plate at Peter. "You do what you want with it, but I gotta give it to you."

For a moment, Peter stood frozen, motionless. Then he reached out and took the plate.

"Okay, mister. Take it easy now." Once again, just before he walked off, the old man winked at her.

Holding the license plate, Peter stood alone, staring back across the junk yard at the big black car with the smashed windows that had been his. In a short time he would stop looking, would turn away. He would take the license plate downtown with him and put it in a drawer in his apartment. She would not be there in the apartment with him; before that they would have said good-bye. How far away from her he had chosen to stand, how separate they were from each other. But I know who you are, she thought, I know who you are. I see you, Peter.

They walked until they came to the bridge. They found a taxi there. "The first stop will be One hundred sixteenth and Broadway," Peter told the driver. "Then I'll be going down a little farther."

They were sitting side by side in the back seat, and the taxi was taking them over the bridge. If there were something she could say . . . Suddenly she couldn't bear not telling him in some way that she was here with him, that she hadn't come just for the ride, couldn't bear not touching him. She was no longer afraid. She turned to Peter and put her arms around him, held him close to her. "Susan . . ." she heard him say. He buried his face in her hair.

The taxi went on, west through Harlem, then all the way downtown. When it stopped on 116th Street in front of the dorms, she sat very still. Peter looked at her a long time. "Are you getting out?" he said.

"No," she said softly. "Not here."

At 111th Street, the meter read four dollars and twenty-five cents. Peter gave the driver the five-dollar bill and told him to keep the change.

CHAPTER TWENTY-ONE

IT WAS TIME to go.

They lay beside each other on the bed in silence. Only their hands touched, Peter's hand covering hers, pressing it down flat against the mattress—her fingers had started to ache a little. His other hand held a cigarette. He had gotten out of bed before to get it, had walked all the way across the room to the chair where his jacket was, and she had almost cried out, "No! Not yet!" but the end had already begun. Now she lay watching the wisps of smoke drift up toward the ceiling. The world was returning to her—coming in through the open window. She remembered that she had a train to catch, suitcases to pick up four blocks away, and a door to close for the last time. She was slipping away from Peter, just as he was slipping away from her. This was the end of something that had been completed.

If only there were time enough she would have liked to have fallen asleep. But it was almost two. She would get up and go quickly before there were too many words. Words would have such a heaviness. There had only been one moment when she had felt strange, unsure—it was when they first lay down on the bed together. He had looked at her before he touched her and said, "You've taken everything off." She had known then that it wasn't going to be the same for him.

But when his mouth was on her mouth there had been a rightness about it, a rightness when his body had entered hers . . . and then there had come a time when she had felt herself becoming flooded with light, and she had floated up, up—toward something she had almost reached.

Slowly, she slid her hand from Peter's.

"Is it getting late?" he said.

"I'll have to get dressed."

They lay beside each other for a moment longer. Suddenly he sat up. Turning away from her, he put out his cigarette. "I'll walk you back to the dorms," he said. There was a hollow, remote sound about his voice.

"Peter, why don't you stay here?" she said gently. "Maybe you'll go to sleep."

His eyes were ice-colored when he looked at her. "Maybe that is what I want."

Letting the sheet slip away from her, she sat up.

"Susan." Peter said her name half to himself, as if there were something he was trying to remember. Then he touched her hair. "Your hair is quite long," he said, "after all."

But who do you think I am? she thought. "Goodbye," she whispered, because that was the only thing left to say now.

She got out of bed and put on her clothes—the white bra, the white slip, the white pants, the white dress. It didn't take very long. She went to the mirror that hung above the bureau and began to pull a comb through her hair. There was a girl in the mirror with a clear-eyed, still look, who didn't smile this time. She could see Peter in the mirror too—sitting up alone in the bed, watching her. It was he who had tangled her hair, given her a different face. She felt an aching sadness for him, but none, none at all, for herself. It was hard for her to think the word "love" without shyness, but maybe there were other names for love. Maybe even "good-bye" was a name for it.

"I'm ready," she said at last, putting the comb down.

He had gotten up for another cigarette—was he afraid his face would be naked without one? Now he walked over to her and took her hand. "You're in such a hurry," he said. "Shall I say *bon voyage*? Is that appropriate?" His hand tightened on hers. "I suppose you'd hate me if I said thank you."

"Yes," she said, "I think I would."

He laughed a little painfully. "I didn't even take you to a beach," he said, "though it wouldn't have been much fun in the rain." For a moment he was silent. Then he said, "I didn't even make you come—I wanted to do that."

"It was good anyway," she said. But his face had gone blank and she knew he didn't believe her. "It was what it meant," she said. "I knew what it *meant*."

"Let me at least walk you to the door," he said.

They walked out of the bedroom and down the hall and neither of them tried to say anything. He was still holding her hand. At the door, she turned and faced him and he kissed her. "Good-bye, Peter," she said.

He let her go, opened the door for her. But just as she was leaving, he cried out, "Susan! You don't regret it, do you?"

She looked at Peter for the last time and didn't answer.

"You know," he said, "you must never regret any thing."

"I know," she said.

And then she went.

ABOUT THE AUTHOR

Joyce Johnson was born in 1935 in New York City, the setting for all her fiction: *Come and Join the Dance*, recognized as the first Beat novel by a woman writer, *Bad Connections*, and *In the Night Café*. She is best known for her memoir *Minor Characters*, which won the National Book Critics Circle Award in 1983 and dealt with coming of age in the 1950s and with her involvement with Jack Kerouac. She has published two other Beat-related books: *Door Wide Open: A Beat Love Affair in Letters*, and *The Voice Is All: The Lonely Victory of Jack Kerouac*. She has also written a second memoir, *Missing Men,* and the nonfiction title *What Lisa Knew: The Truths and Lies of the Steinberg Case*.

EBOOKS BY JOYCE JOHNSON

FROM OPEN ROAD MEDIA

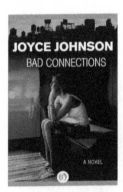
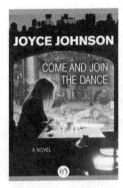
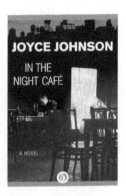

Available wherever ebooks are sold

OPEN ROAD

INTEGRATED MEDIA

Open Road Integrated Media is a digital publisher and multimedia content company. Open Road creates connections between authors and their audiences by marketing its ebooks through a new proprietary online platform, which uses premium video content and social media.